by Liam O'Donnell
illustrated by Janek Matysiak

Librarian Reviewer
Joanne Bongaarts
Educational Consultant
MS in Library Media Education, Minnesota State University, Mankato
Teacher and Media Specialist with Edina Public Schools, MN, 1993–2000

Reading Consultant
Elizabeth Stedem
Educator/Consultant, Colorado Springs, CO
M.A. in Elementary Education, University of Denver, CO

STONE ARCH BOOKS
Minneapolis San Diego

First published in the United States in 2007
by Stone Arch Books,
151 Good Counsel Drive, P.O. Box 669,
Mankato, Minnesota 56002.
www.stonearchbooks.com

Originally published in Great Britain in 2000
by A & C Black Publishers Ltd,
38 Soho Square, London, W1D 3HB.

Library of Congress Cataloging-in-Publication Data
O'Donnell, Liam, 1970–
System Shock / by Liam O'Donnell; illustrated by Janek Matysiak.
p. cm. — (Graphic Quest)
ISBN-13: 978-1-59889-083-9 (hardcover)
ISBN-10: 1-59889-083-2 (hardcover)
ISBN-13: 978-1-59889-214-7 (paperback)
ISBN-10: 1-59889-214-2 (paperback)
1. Graphic novels. I. Matysiak, Janek. II. Title. III. Series.
PN6733.O36S98 2007
741.5'971—dc22 2006007185

Summary: In the distant future, Daniel, Jack, and Jemma find themselves trapped in a virtual reality world. If they don't find a way out soon, they are in danger of being erased forever!

Art Director: Heather Kindseth
Colorists: Kathy Clobes and Mary Bode
Graphic Designer: Brann Garvey
Production Artist: Keegan Gilbert

1 2 3 4 5 6 11 10 09 08 07 06

Printed in the United States of America.

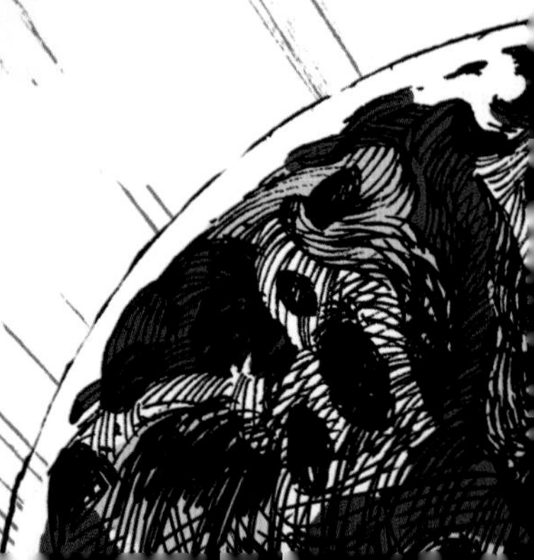

table of CONTENTS

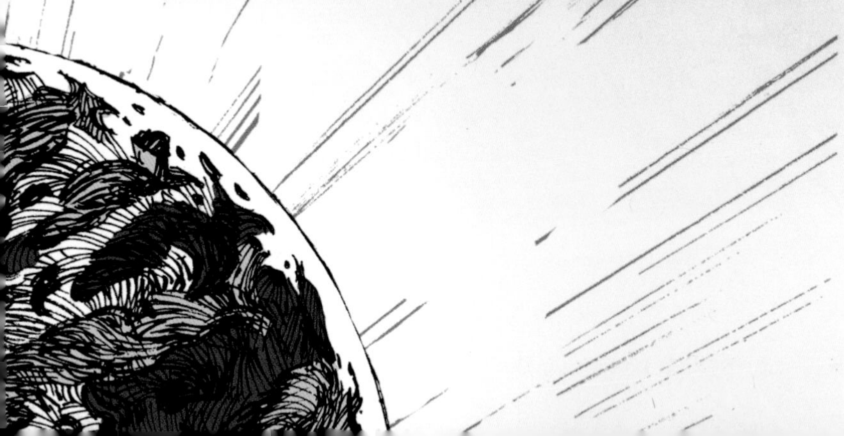

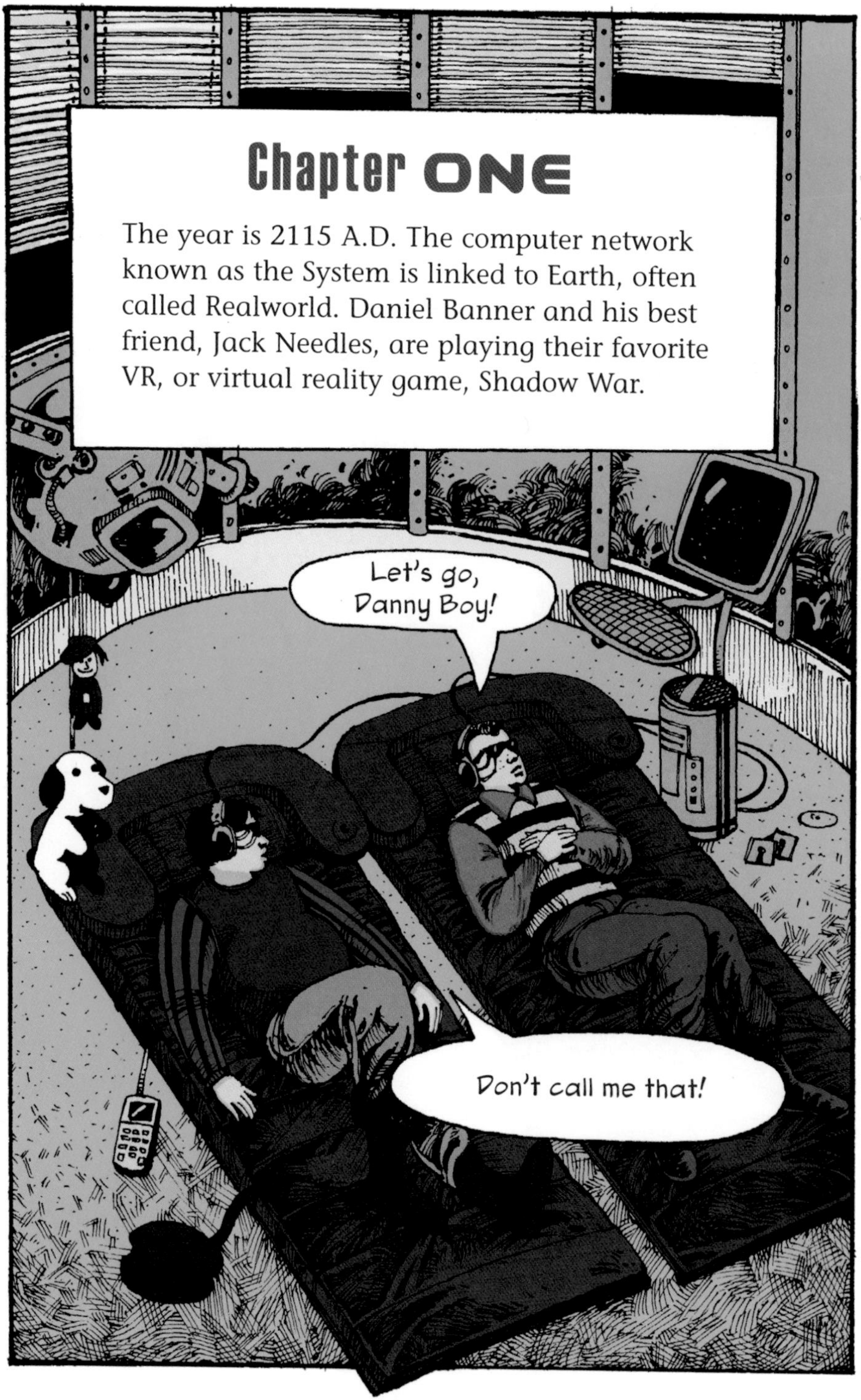
Chapter ONE
The year is 2115 A.D. The computer network known as the System is linked to Earth, often called Realworld. Daniel Banner and his best friend, Jack Needles, are playing their favorite VR, or virtual reality game, Shadow War.
Let's go, Danny Boy!
Don't call me that!

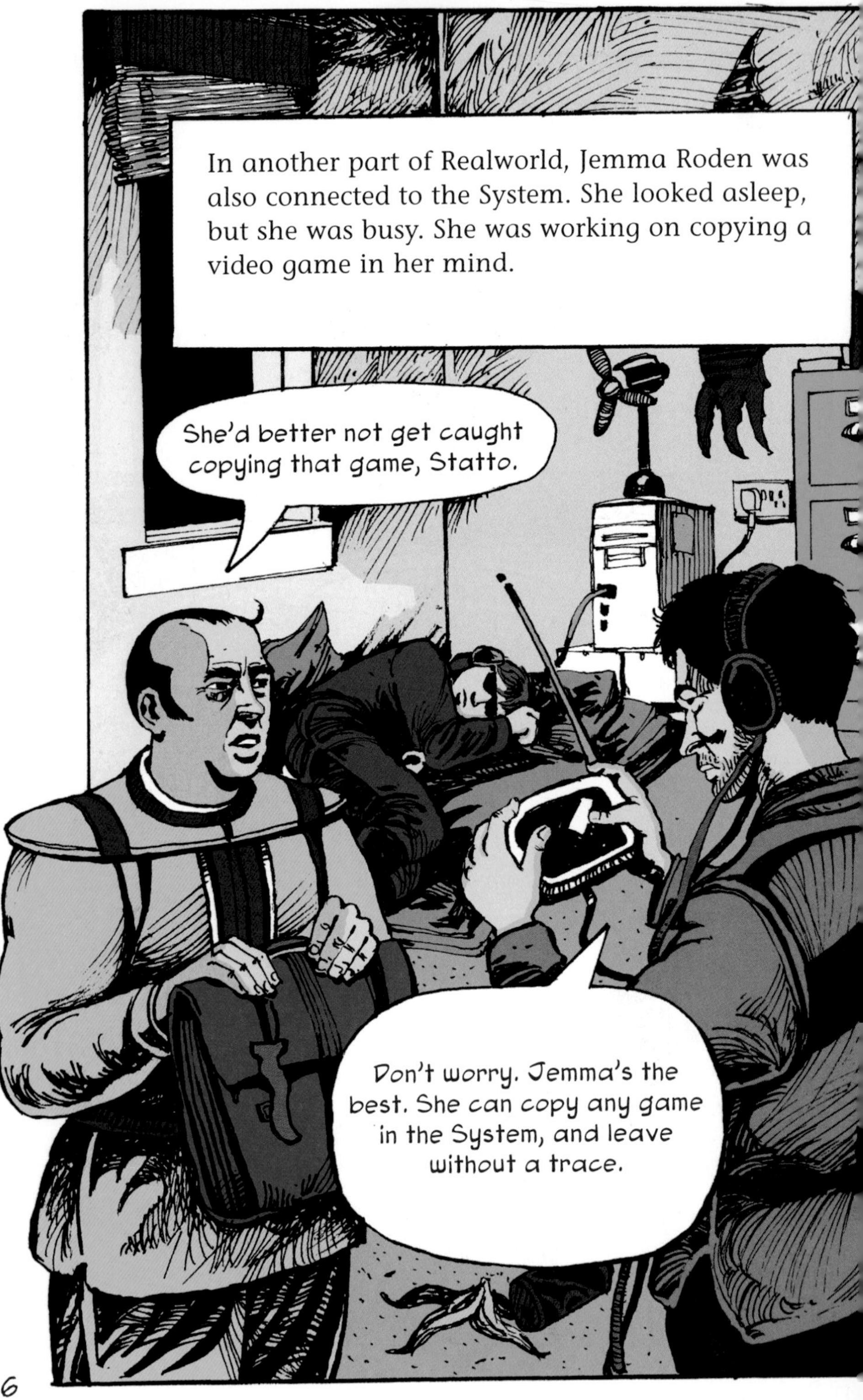
In another part of Realworld, Jemma Roden was also connected to the System. She looked asleep, but she was busy. She was working on copying a video game in her mind.
She'd better not get caught copying that game, Statto.
Don't worry. Jemma's the best. She can copy any game in the System, and leave without a trace.

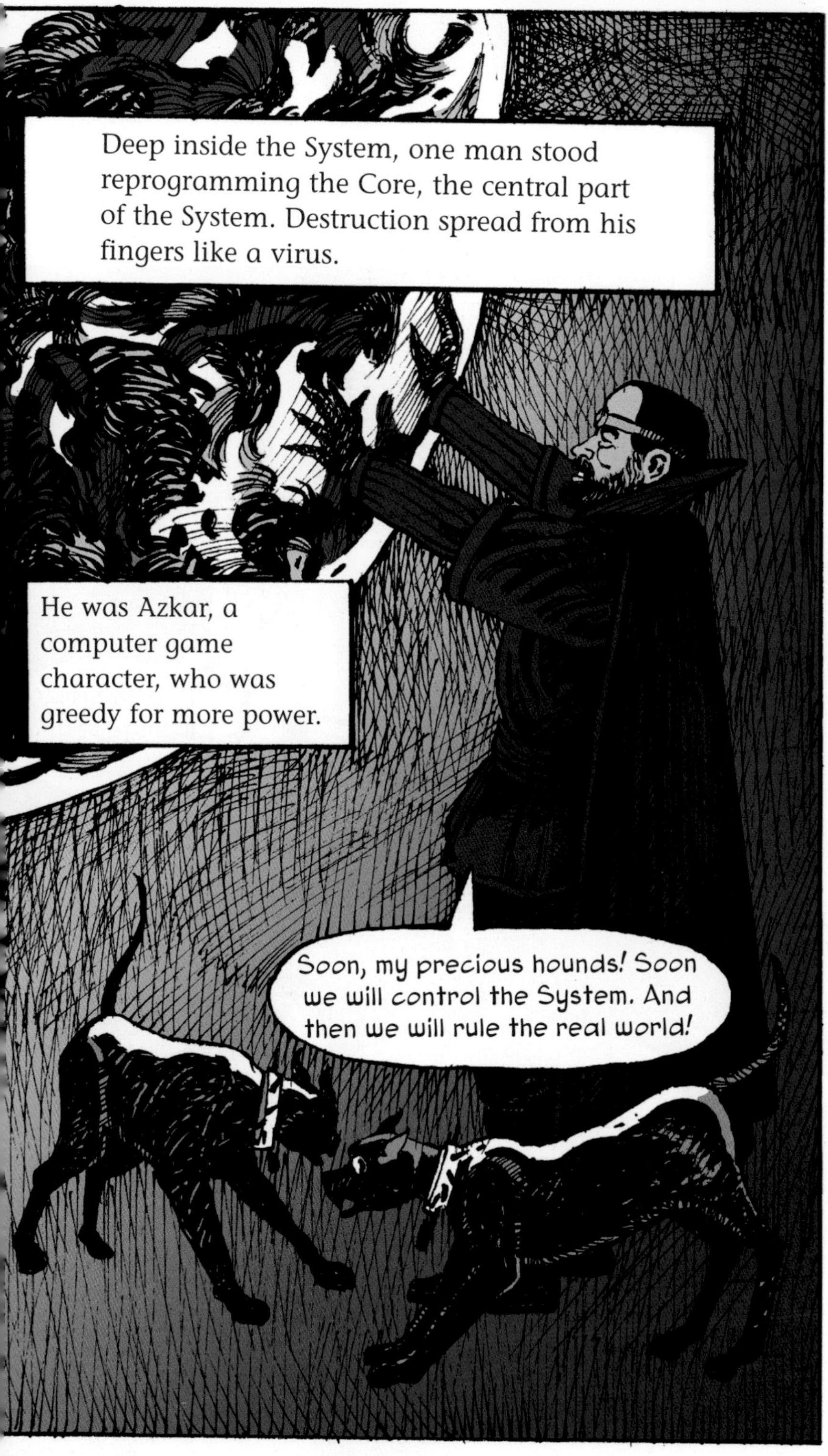
Deep inside the System, one man stood reprogramming the Core, the central part of the System. Destruction spread from his fingers like a virus.
He was Azkar, a computer game character, who was greedy for more power.
Soon, my precious hounds! Soon we will control the System. And then we will rule the real world!

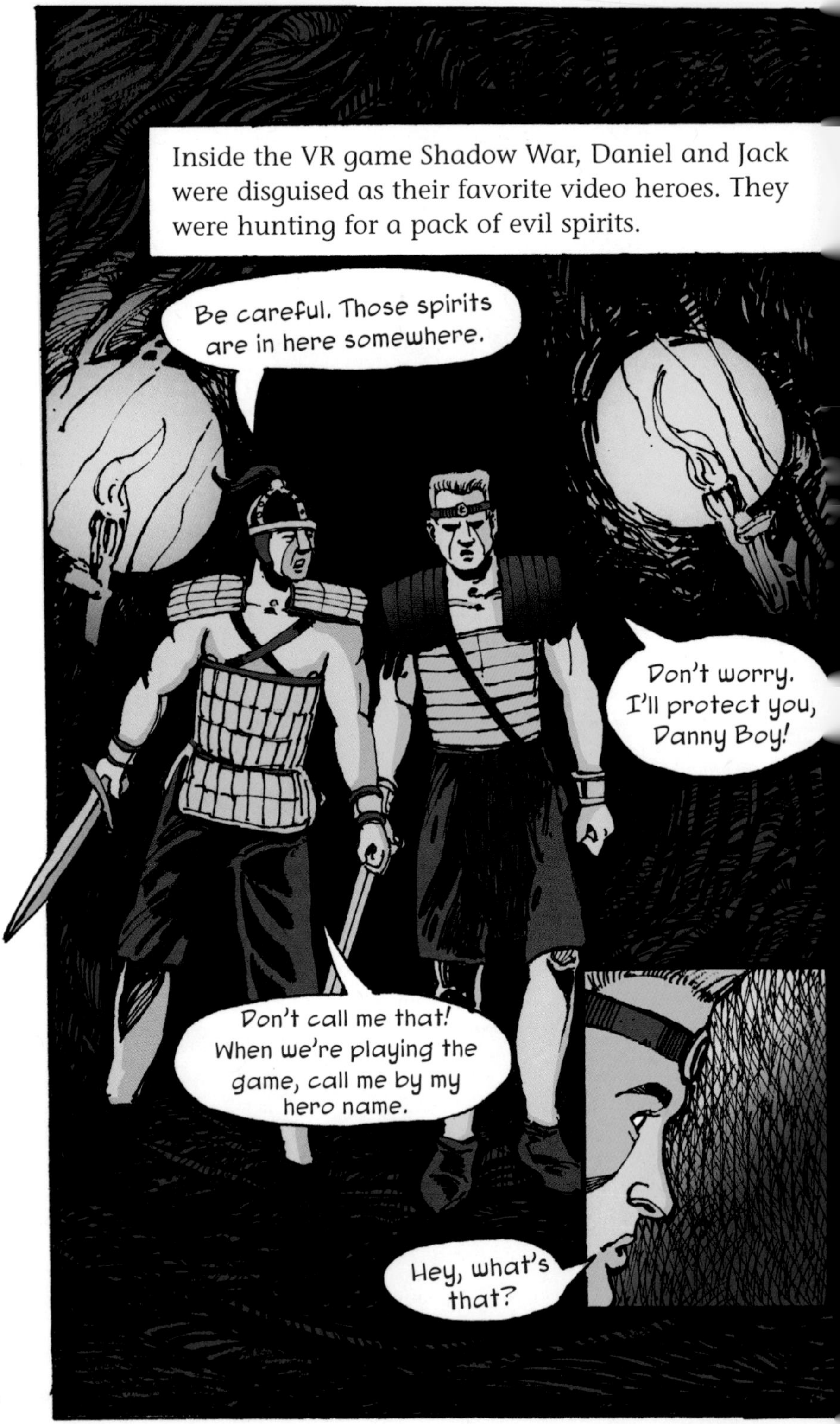
Inside the VR game Shadow War, Daniel and Jack were disguised as their favorite video heroes. They were hunting for a pack of evil spirits.
Be careful. Those spirits are in here somewhere.
Don't worry. I'll protect you, Danny Boy!
Don't call me that! When we're playing the game, call me by my hero name.
Hey, what's that?

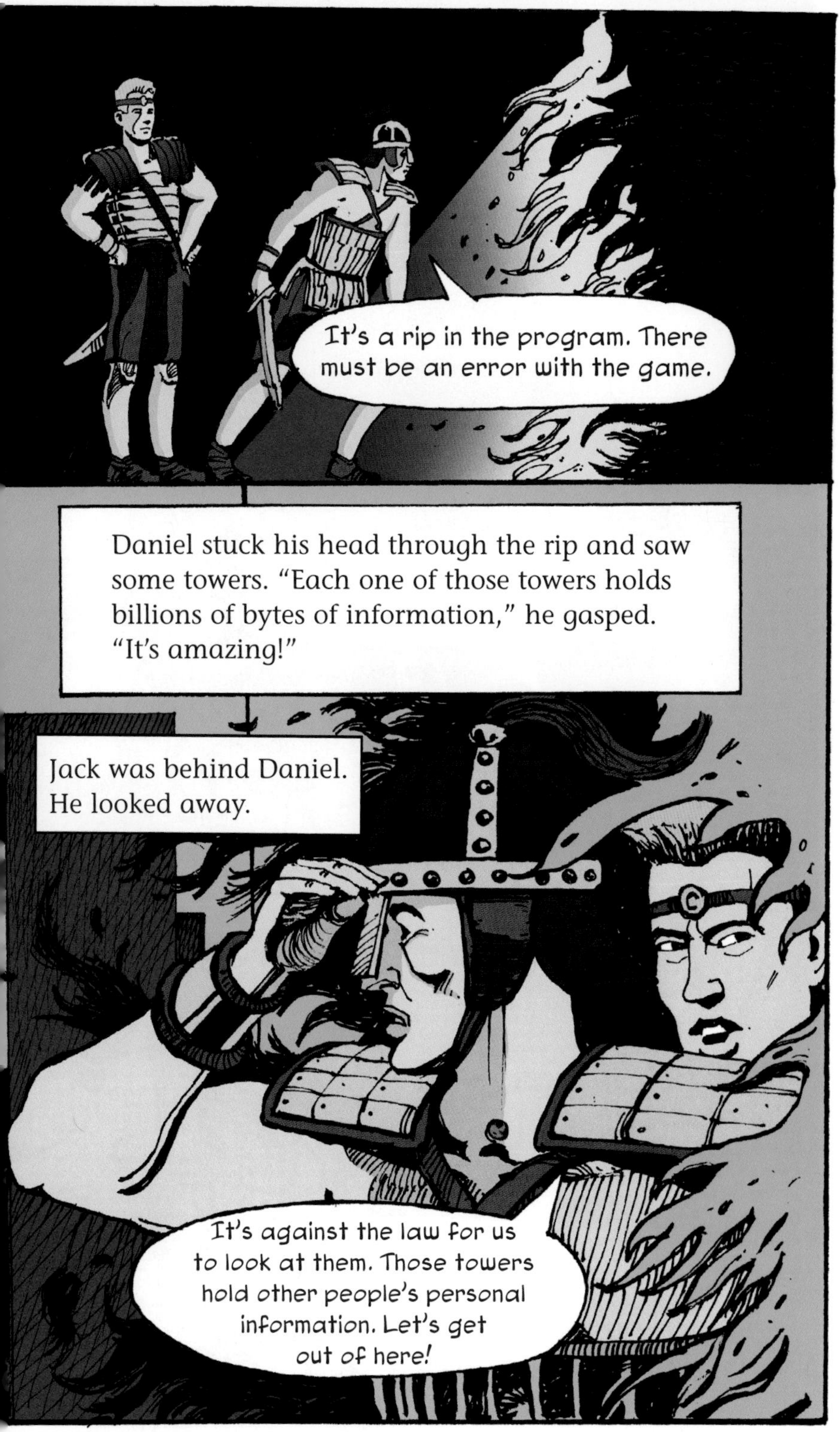
It's a rip in the program. There must be an error with the game.
Daniel stuck his head through the rip and saw some towers. "Each one of those towers holds billions of bytes of information," he gasped. "It's amazing!"
Jack was behind Daniel. He looked away.
It's against the law for us to look at them. Those towers hold other people's personal information. Let's get out of here!

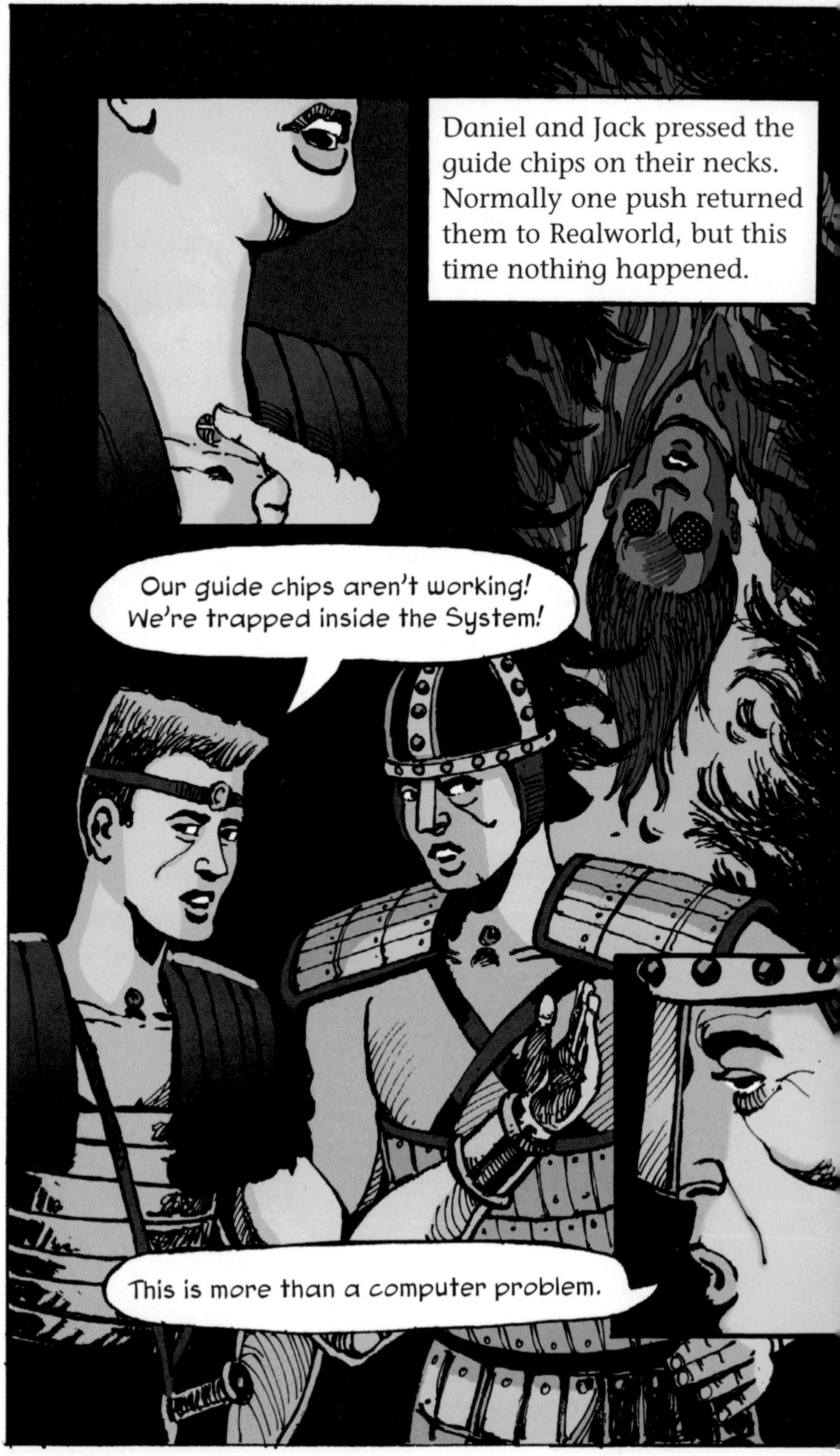
Daniel and Jack pressed the guide chips on their necks. Normally one push returned them to Realworld, but this time nothing happened.
Our guide chips aren't working! We're trapped inside the System!
This is more than a computer problem.

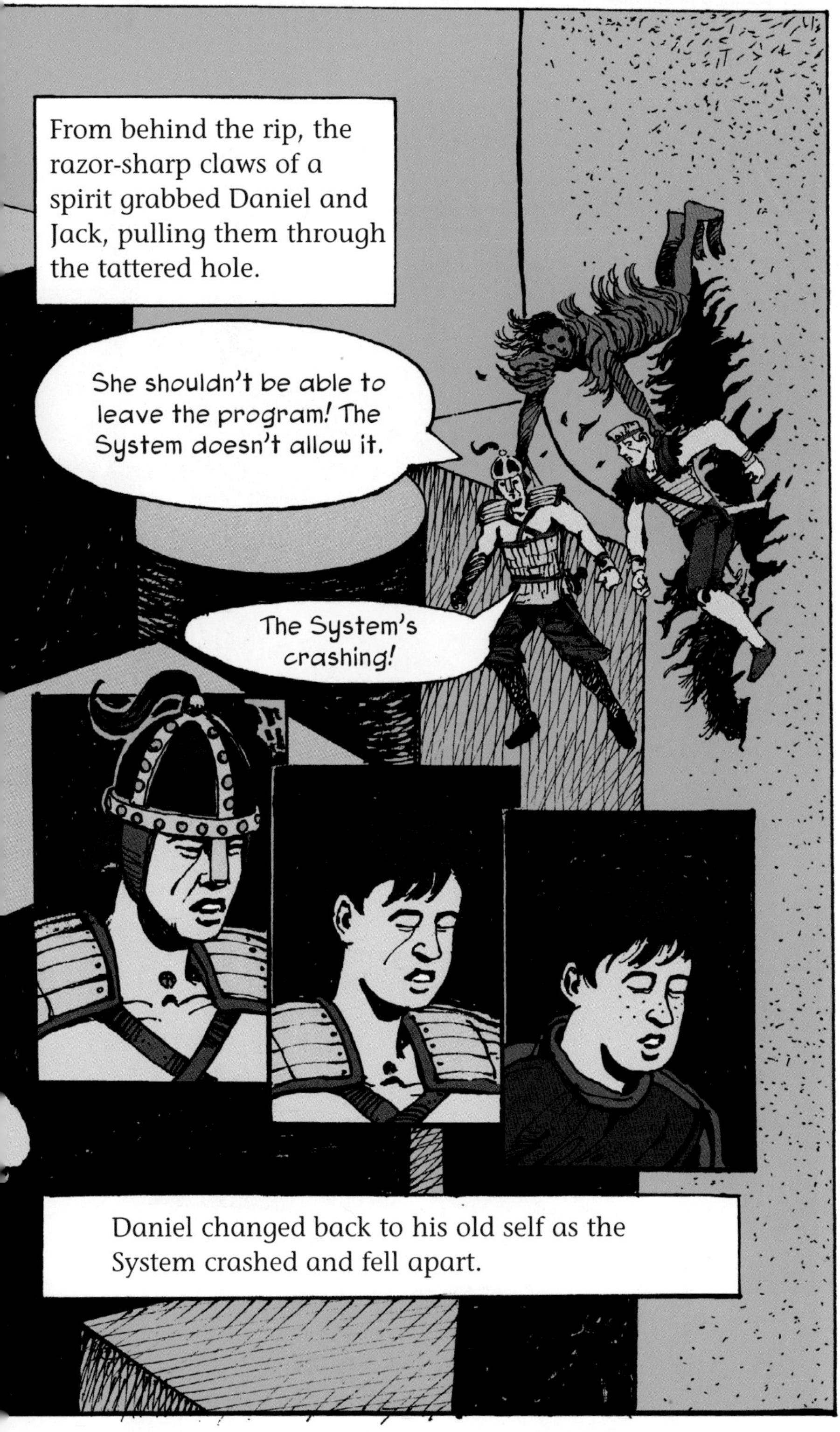
From behind the rip, the razor-sharp claws of a spirit grabbed Daniel and Jack, pulling them through the tattered hole.
She shouldn't be able to leave the program! The System doesn't allow it.
The System's crashing!
Daniel changed back to his old self as the System crashed and fell apart.

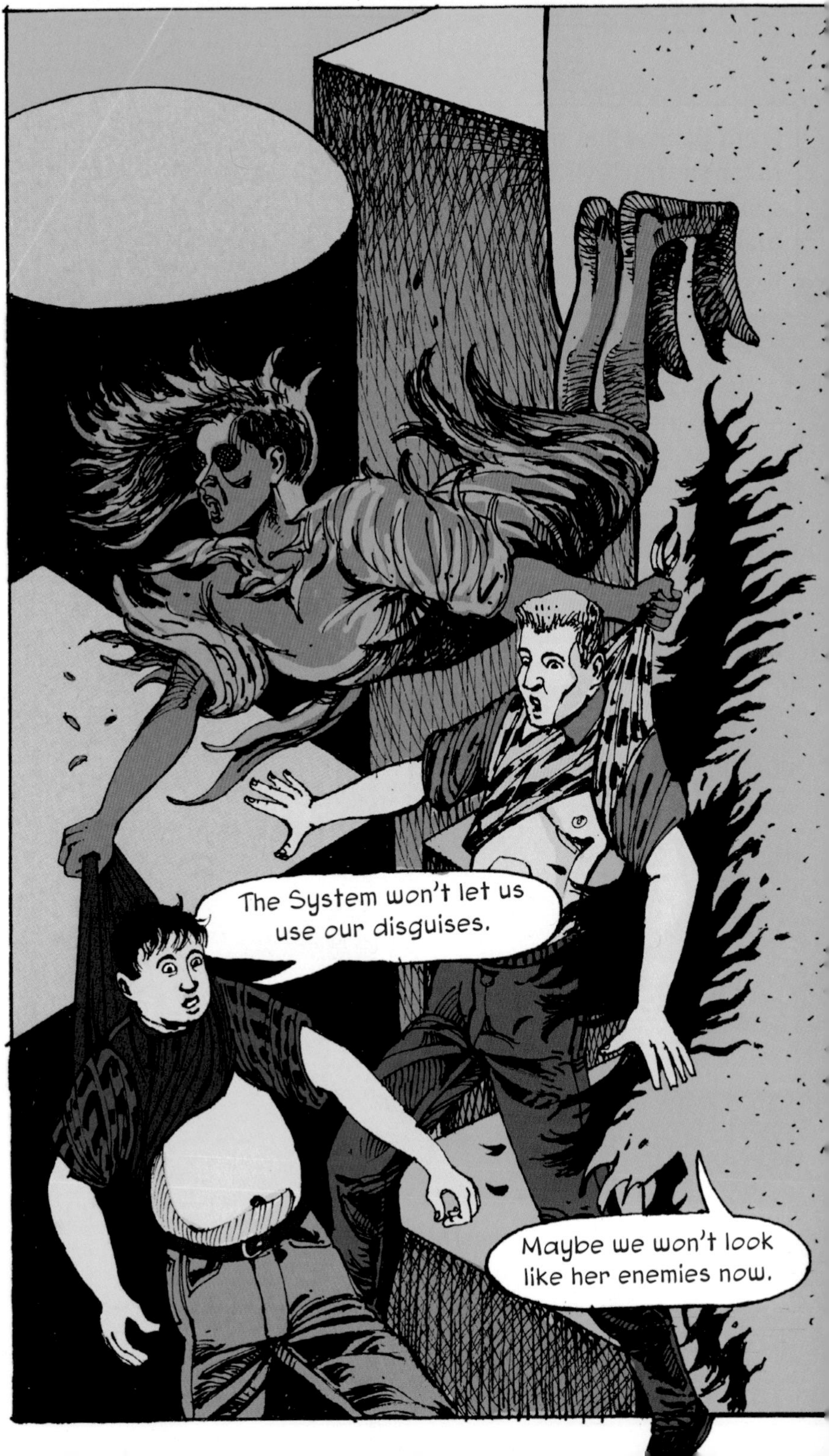
The System won't let us use our disguises.
Maybe we won't look like her enemies now.

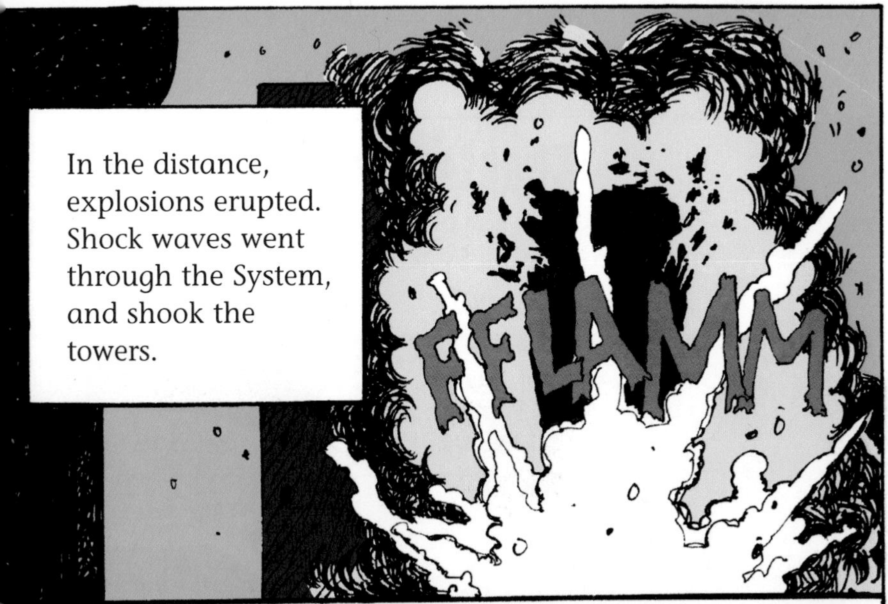
In the distance, explosions erupted. Shock waves went through the System, and shook the towers.
FFLAMM

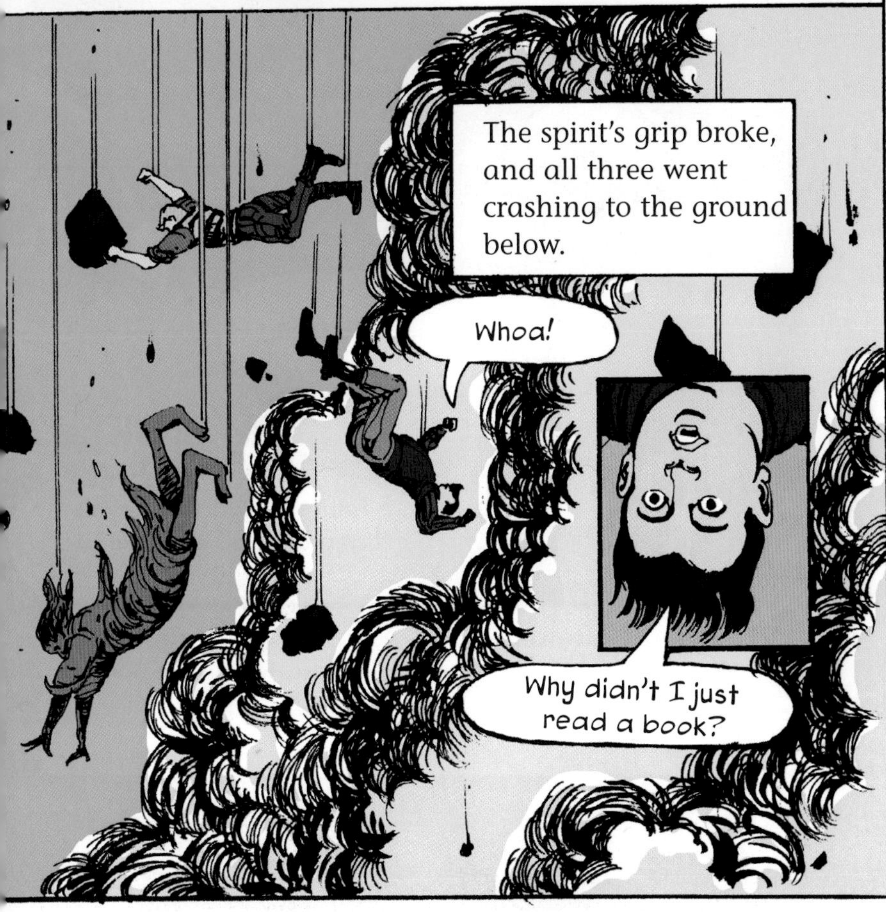
The spirit's grip broke, and all three went crashing to the ground below.
Whoa!
Why didn't I just read a book?

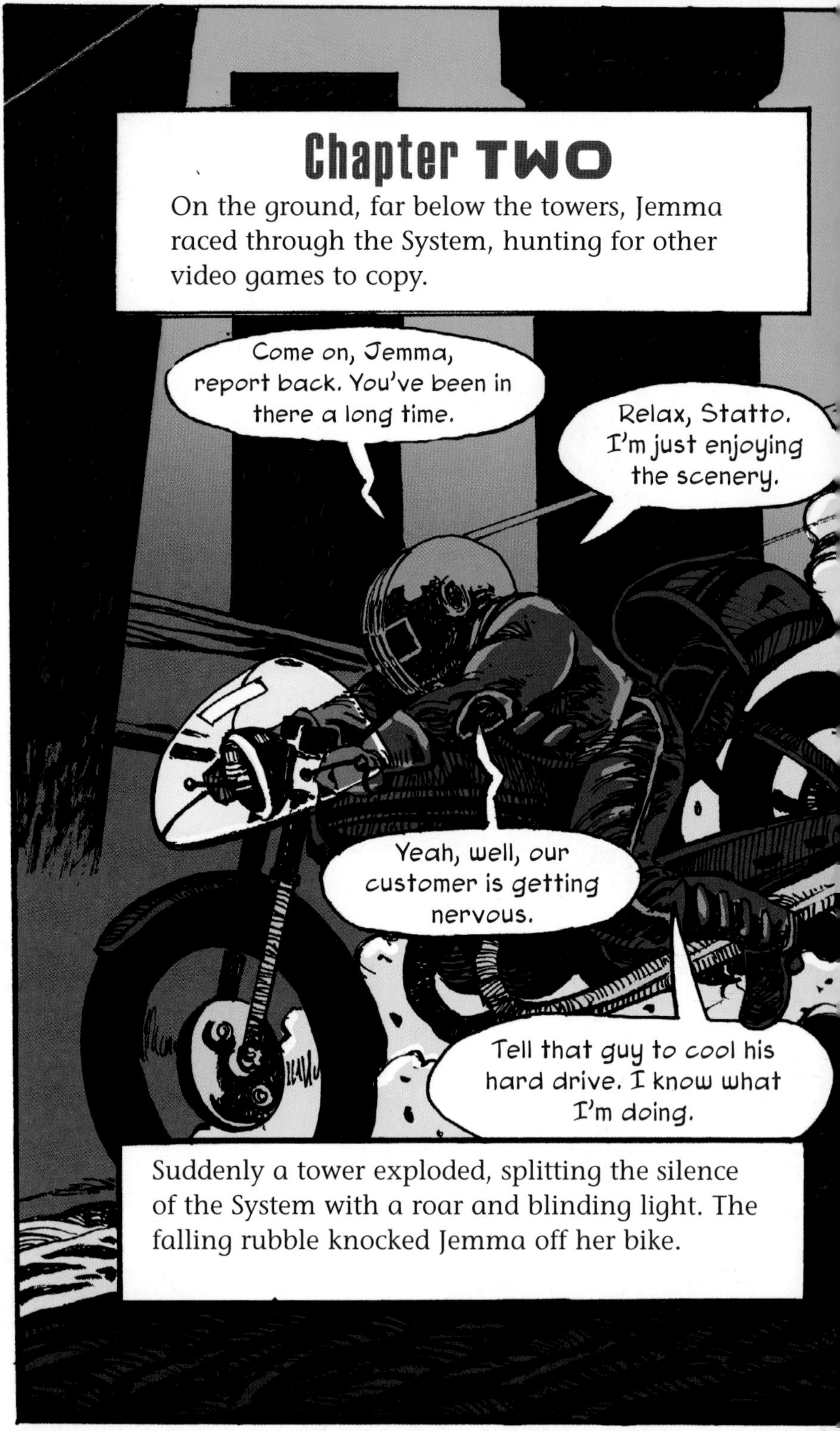
Chapter TWO
On the ground, far below the towers, Jemma raced through the System, hunting for other video games to copy.
Come on, Jemma, report back. You've been in there a long time.
Relax, Statto. I'm just enjoying the scenery.
Yeah, well, our customer is getting nervous.
Tell that guy to cool his hard drive. I know what I'm doing.
Suddenly a tower exploded, splitting the silence of the System with a roar and blinding light. The falling rubble knocked Jemma off her bike.

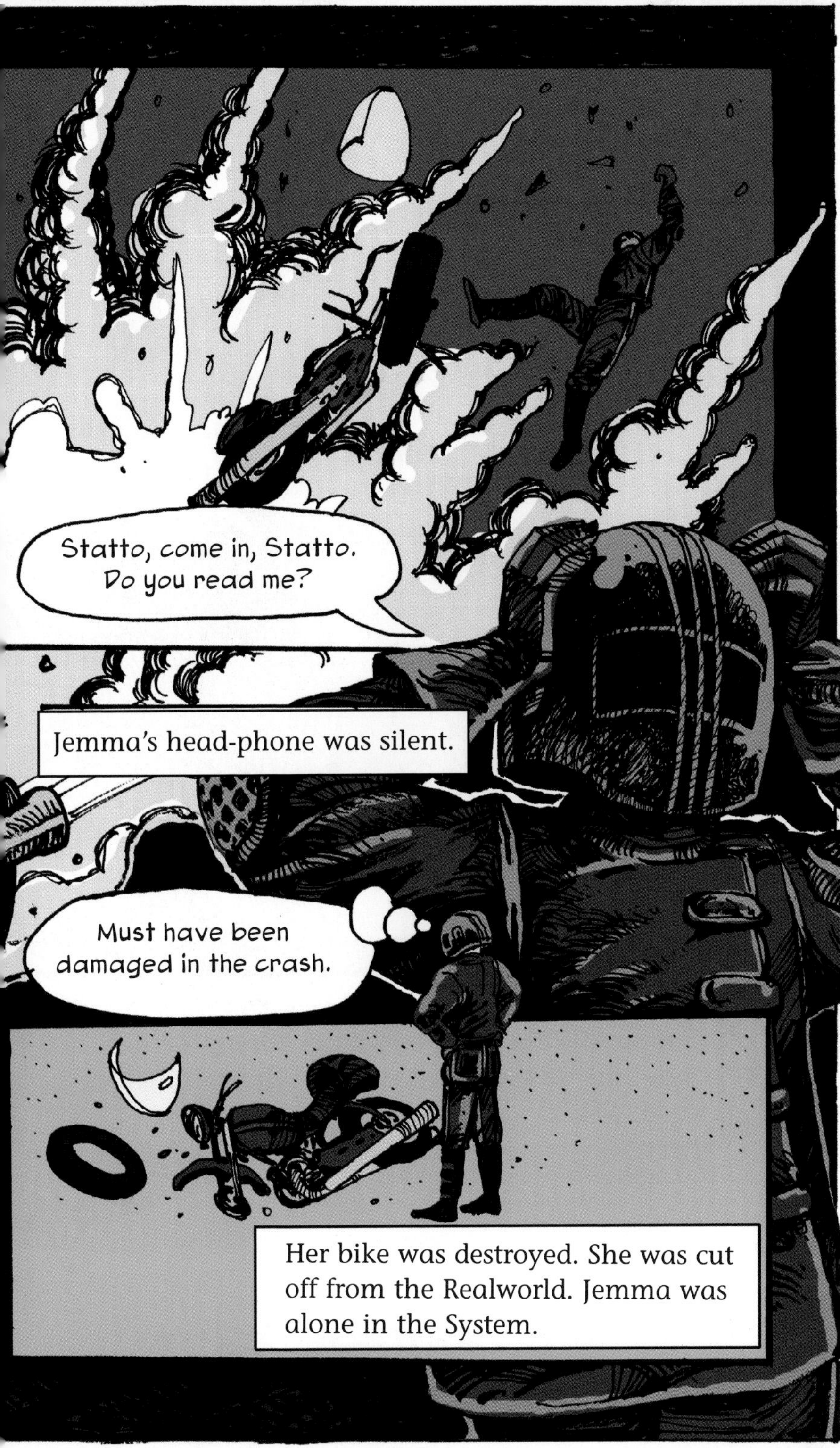
Statto, come in, Statto. Do you read me?
Jemma's head-phone was silent.
Must have been damaged in the crash.
Her bike was destroyed. She was cut off from the Realworld. Jemma was alone in the System.

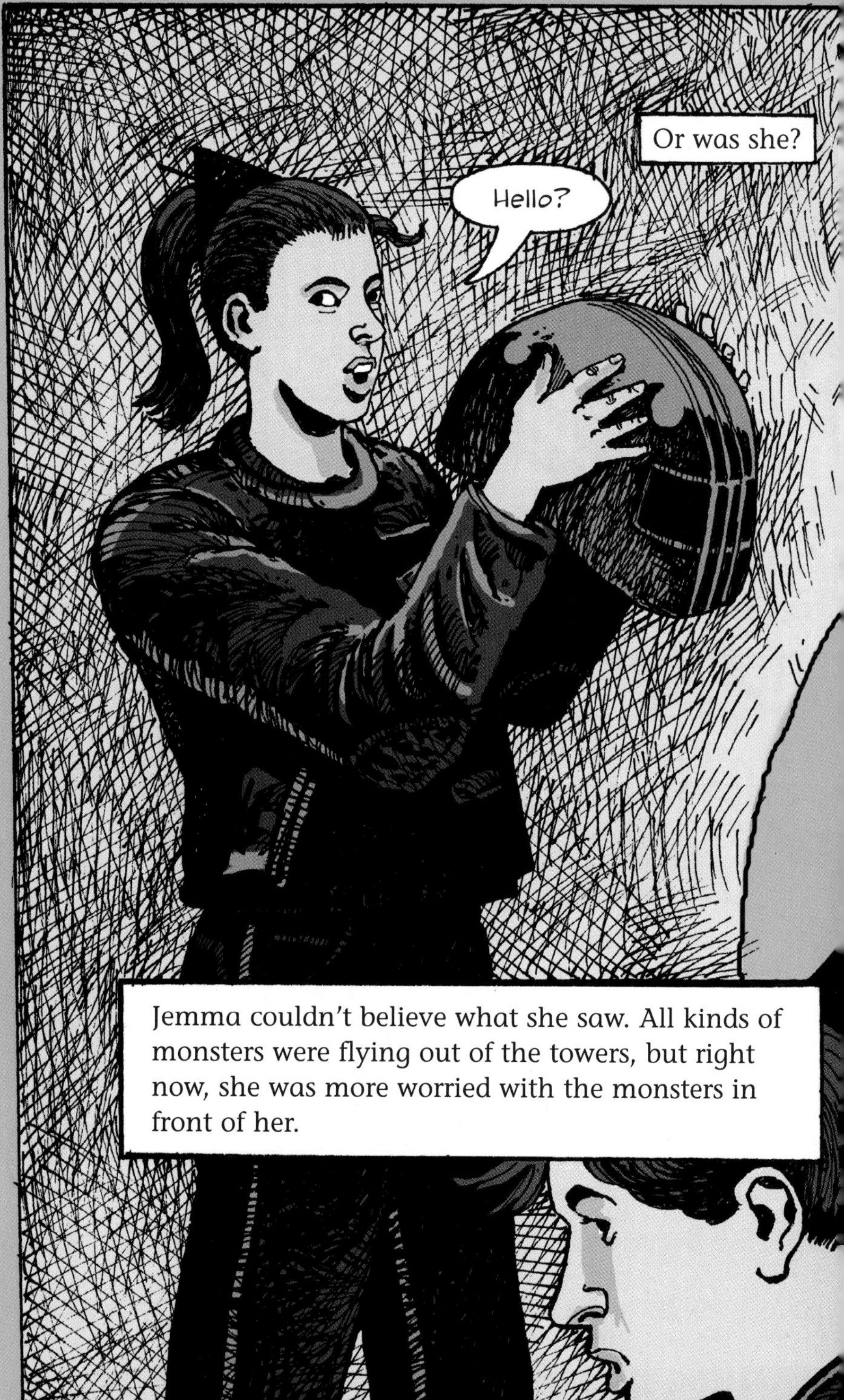
Or was she?
Hello?
Jemma couldn't believe what she saw. All kinds of monsters were flying out of the towers, but right now, she was more worried with the monsters in front of her.

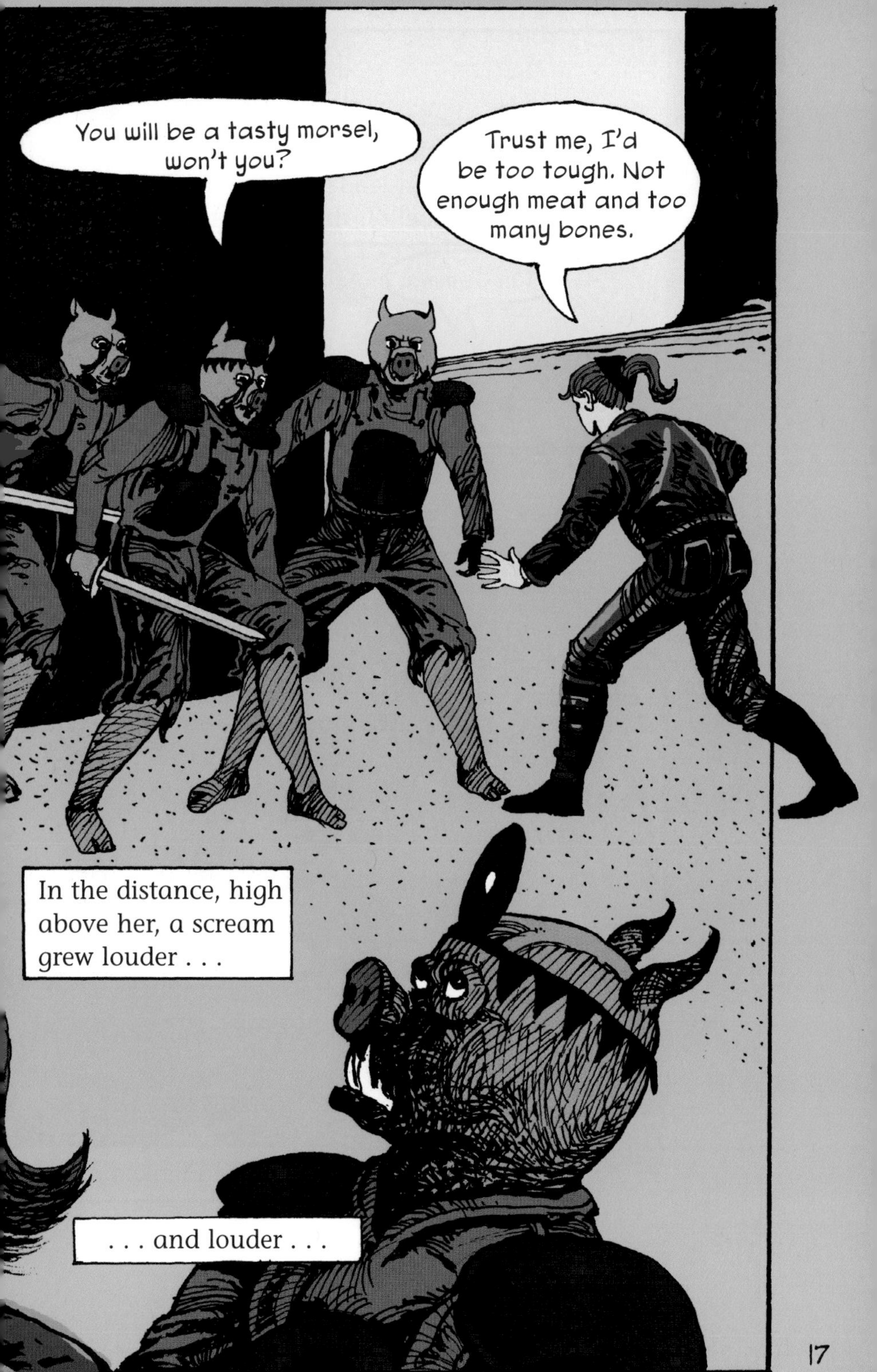
You will be a tasty morsel, won't you?
Trust me, I'd be too tough. Not enough meat and too many bones.
In the distance, high above her, a scream grew louder . . .
. . . and louder . . .

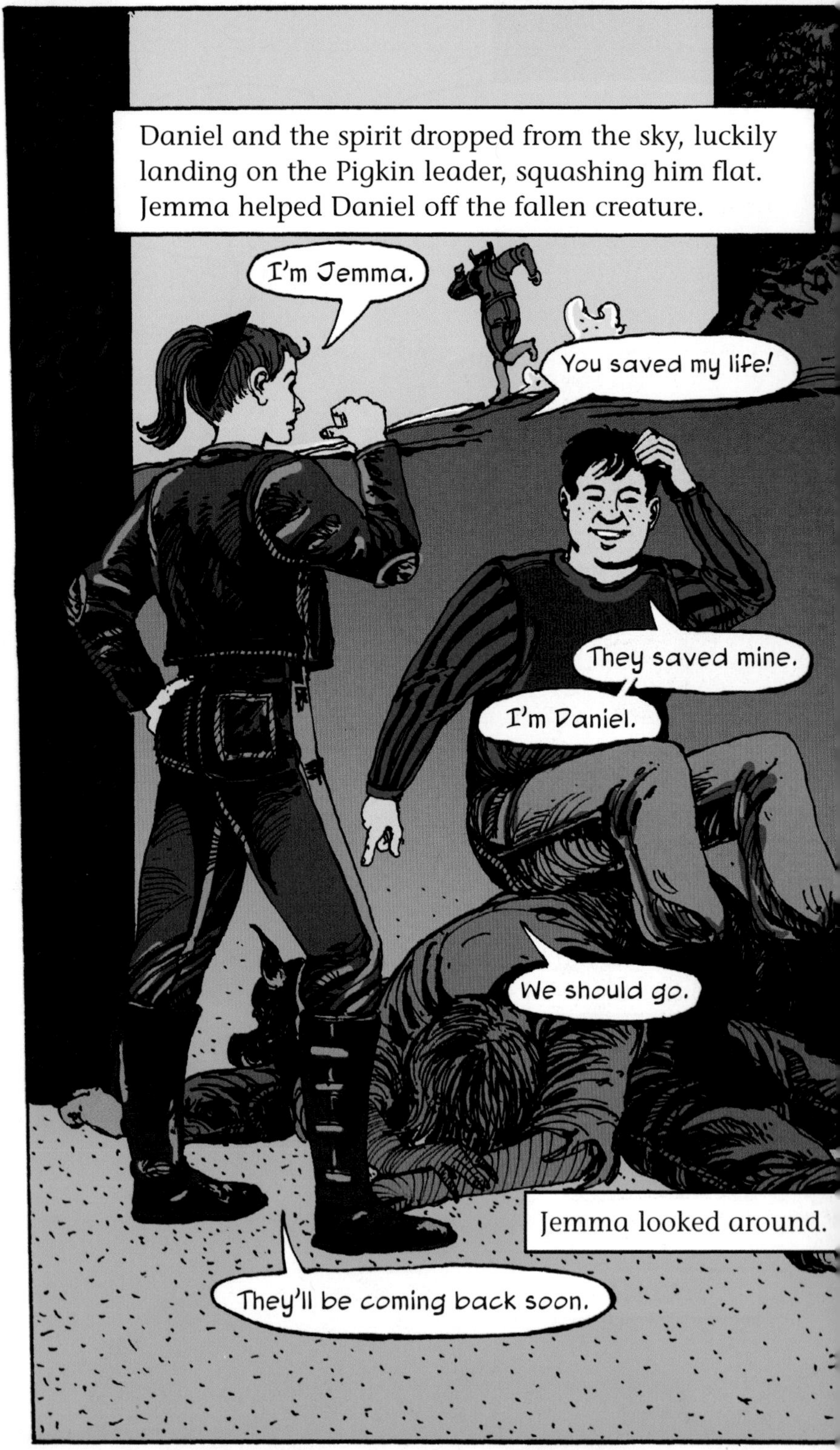
Daniel and the spirit dropped from the sky, luckily landing on the Pigkin leader, squashing him flat. Jemma helped Daniel off the fallen creature.
I'm Jemma.
You saved my life!
They saved mine.
I'm Daniel.
We should go.
Jemma looked around.
They'll be coming back soon.

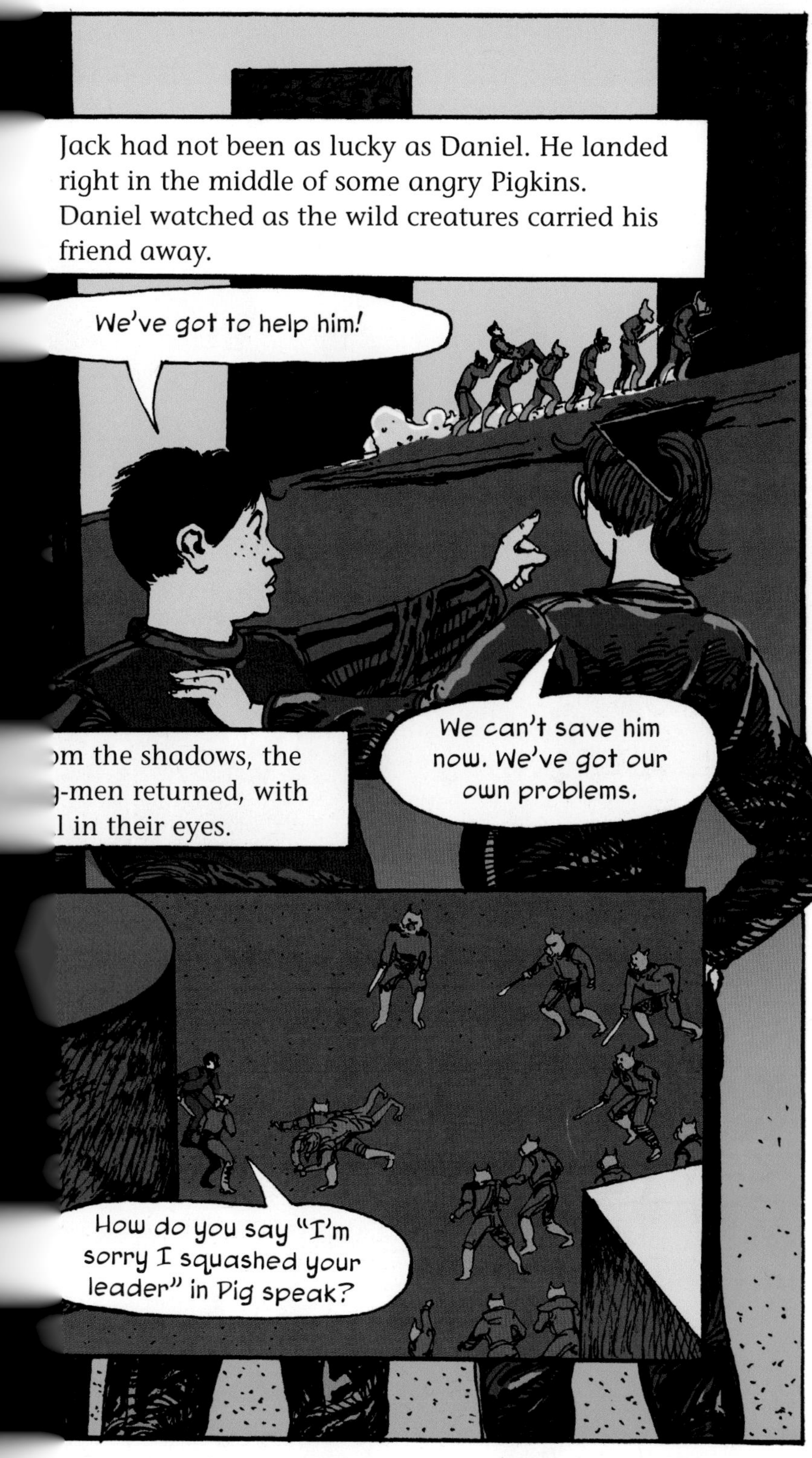
Jack had not been as lucky as Daniel. He landed right in the middle of some angry Pigkins. Daniel watched as the wild creatures carried his friend away.
We've got to help him!
We can't save him now. We've got our own problems.
m the shadows, the
-men returned, with
l in their eyes.
How do you say "I'm sorry I squashed your leader" in Pig speak?

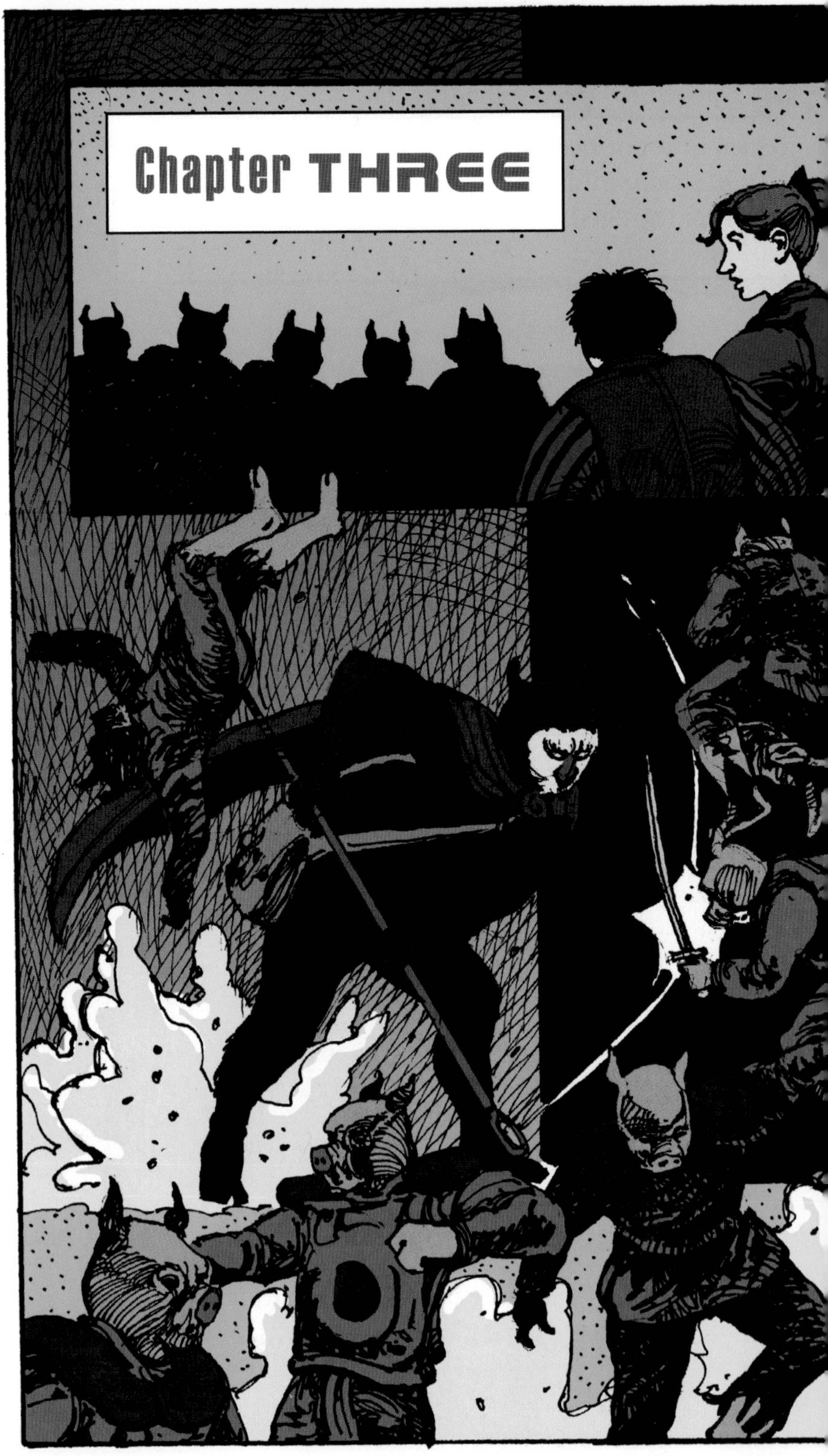
Chapter THREE

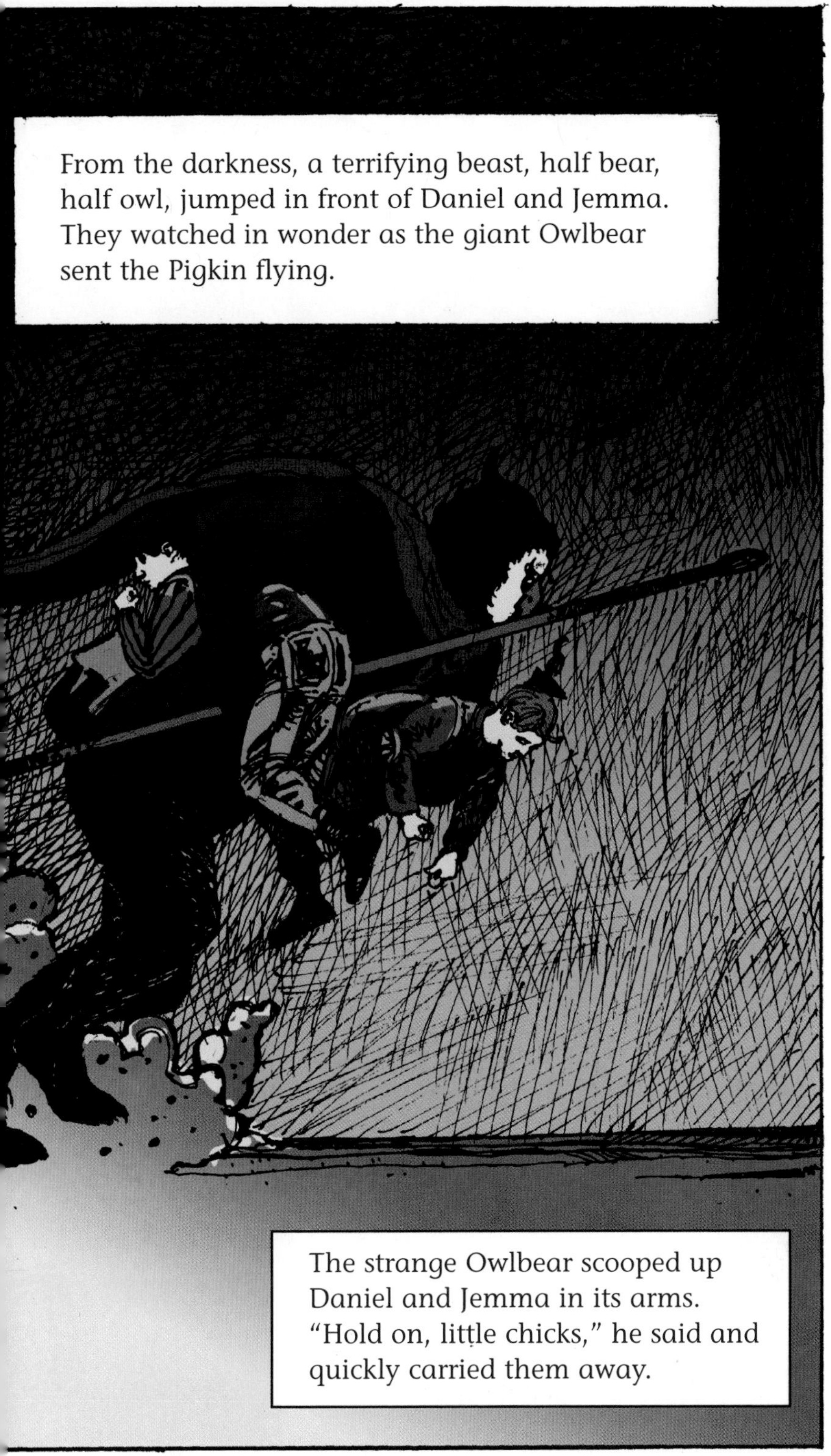
From the darkness, a terrifying beast, half bear, half owl, jumped in front of Daniel and Jemma. They watched in wonder as the giant Owlbear sent the Pigkin flying.
The strange Owlbear scooped up Daniel and Jemma in its arms. "Hold on, little chicks," he said and quickly carried them away.

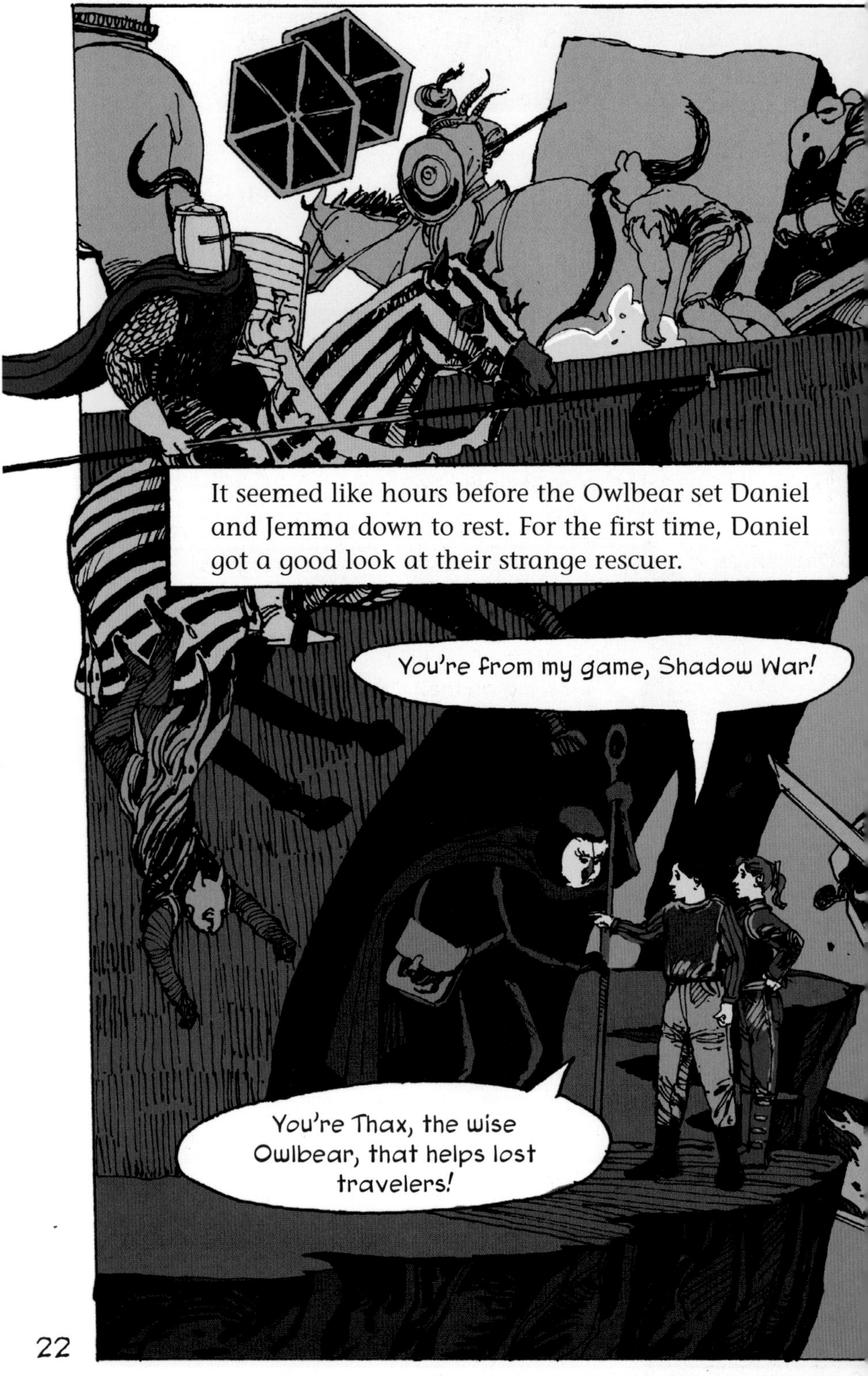
It seemed like hours before the Owlbear set Daniel and Jemma down to rest. For the first time, Daniel got a good look at their strange rescuer.
You're from my game, Shadow War!
You're Thax, the wise Owlbear, that helps lost travelers!

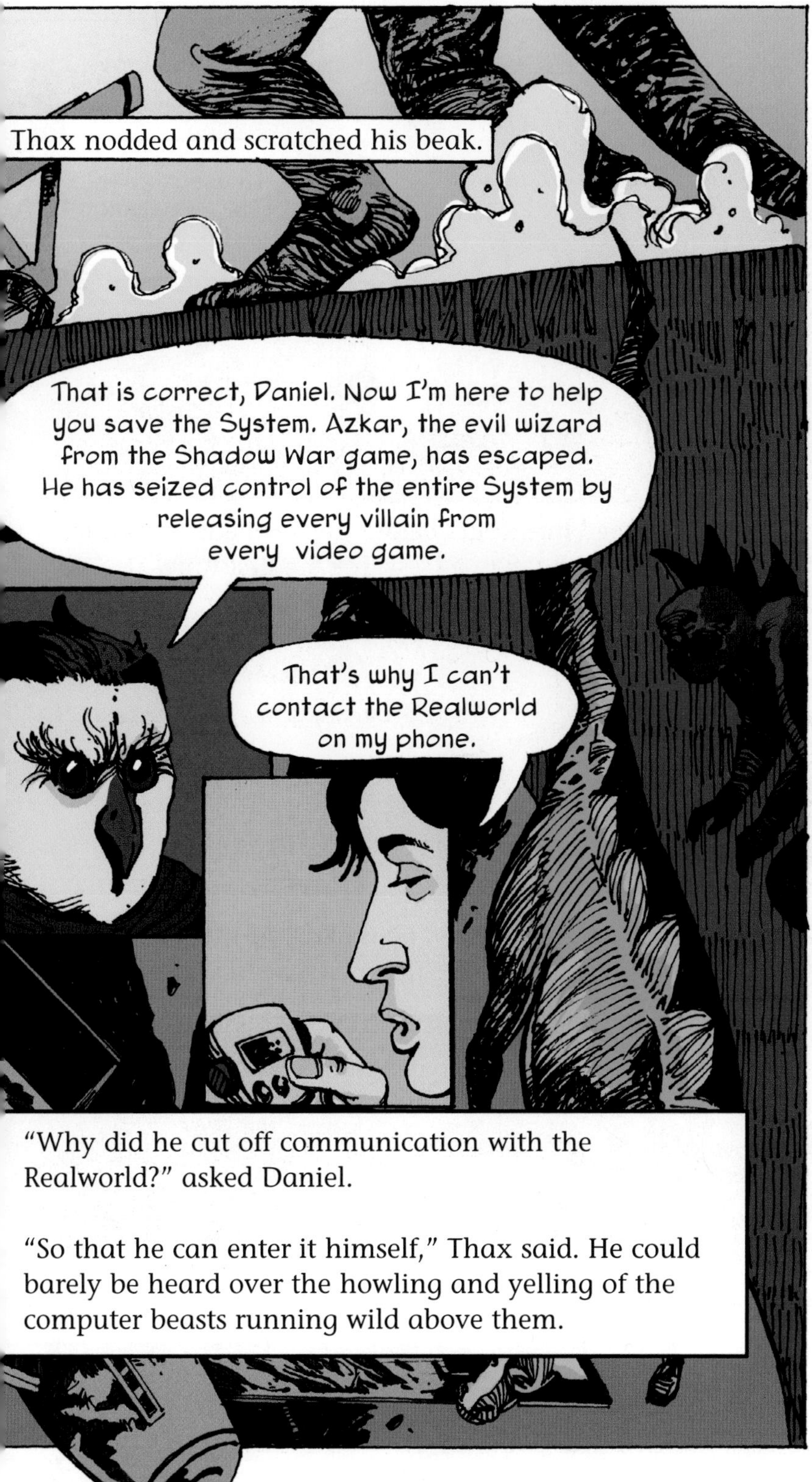
Thax nodded and scratched his beak.
That is correct, Daniel. Now I'm here to help you save the System. Azkar, the evil wizard from the Shadow War game, has escaped. He has seized control of the entire System by releasing every villain from every video game.
That's why I can't contact the Realworld on my phone.
"Why did he cut off communication with the Realworld?" asked Daniel.
"So that he can enter it himself," Thax said. He could barely be heard over the howling and yelling of the computer beasts running wild above them.

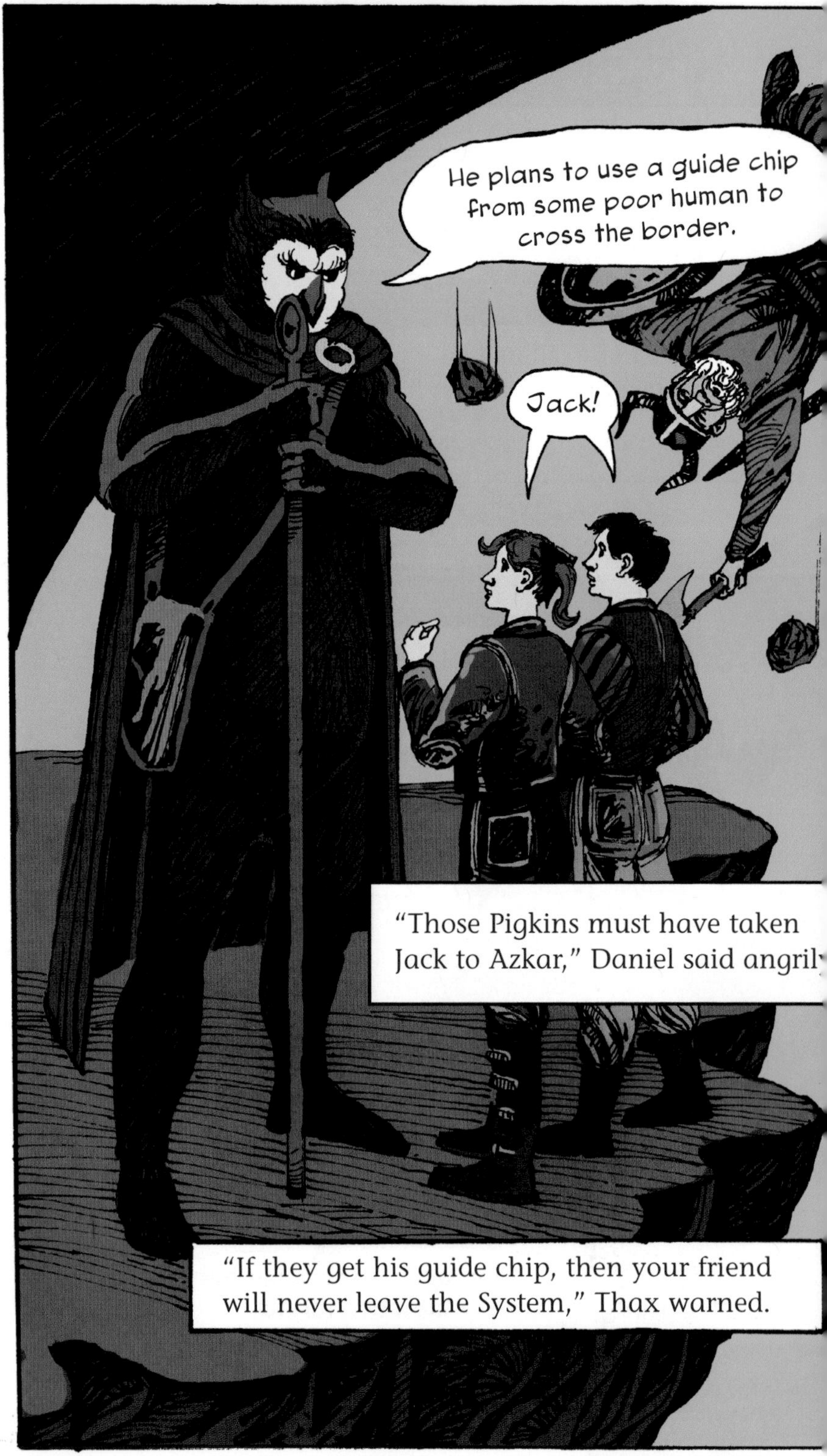
He plans to use a guide chip from some poor human to cross the border.
Jack!
"Those Pigkins must have taken Jack to Azkar," Daniel said angril
"If they get his guide chip, then your friend will never leave the System," Thax warned.

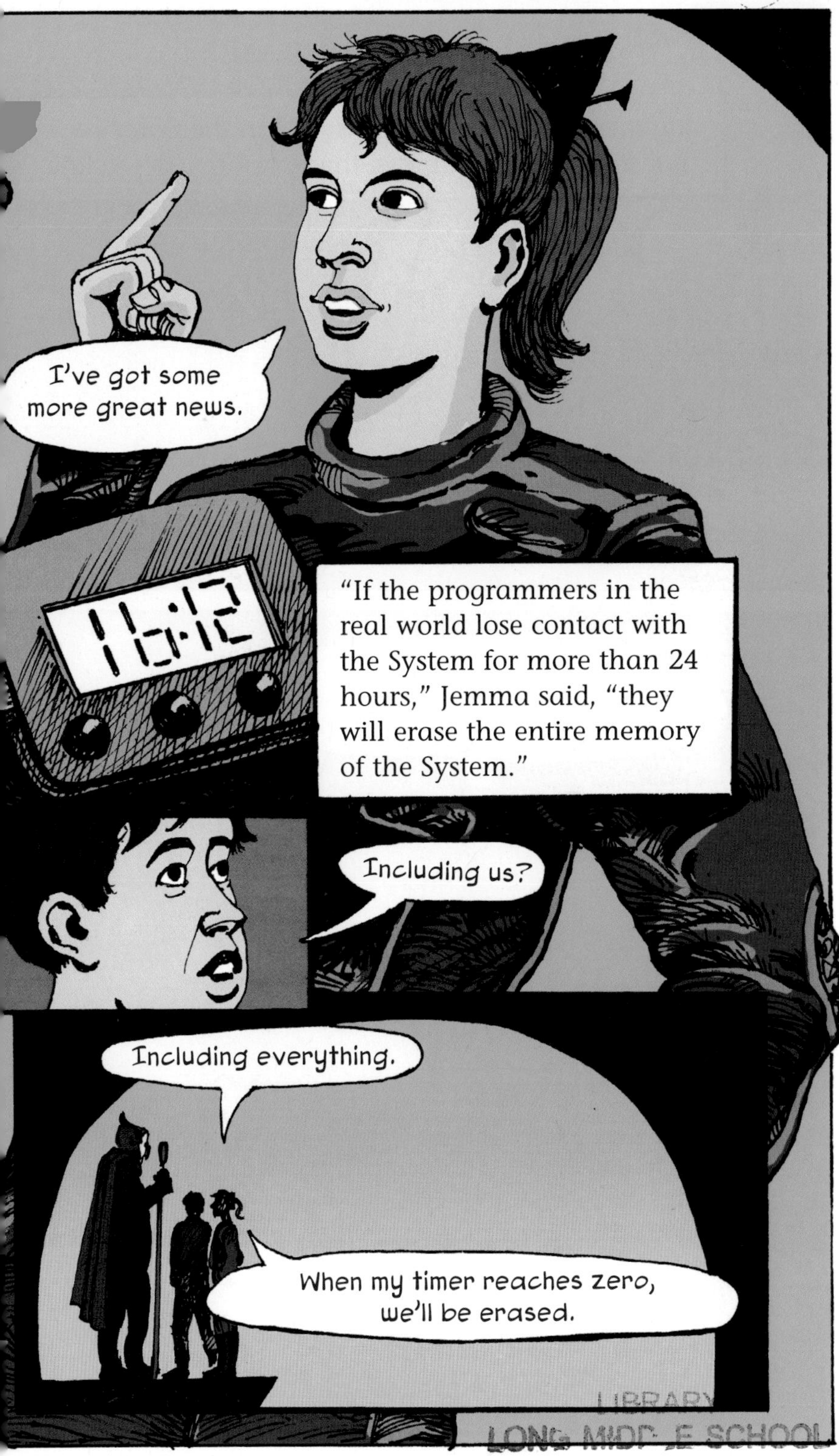
I've got some more great news.
"If the programmers in the real world lose contact with the System for more than 24 hours," Jemma said, "they will erase the entire memory of the System."
Including us?
Including everything.
When my timer reaches zero, we'll be erased.

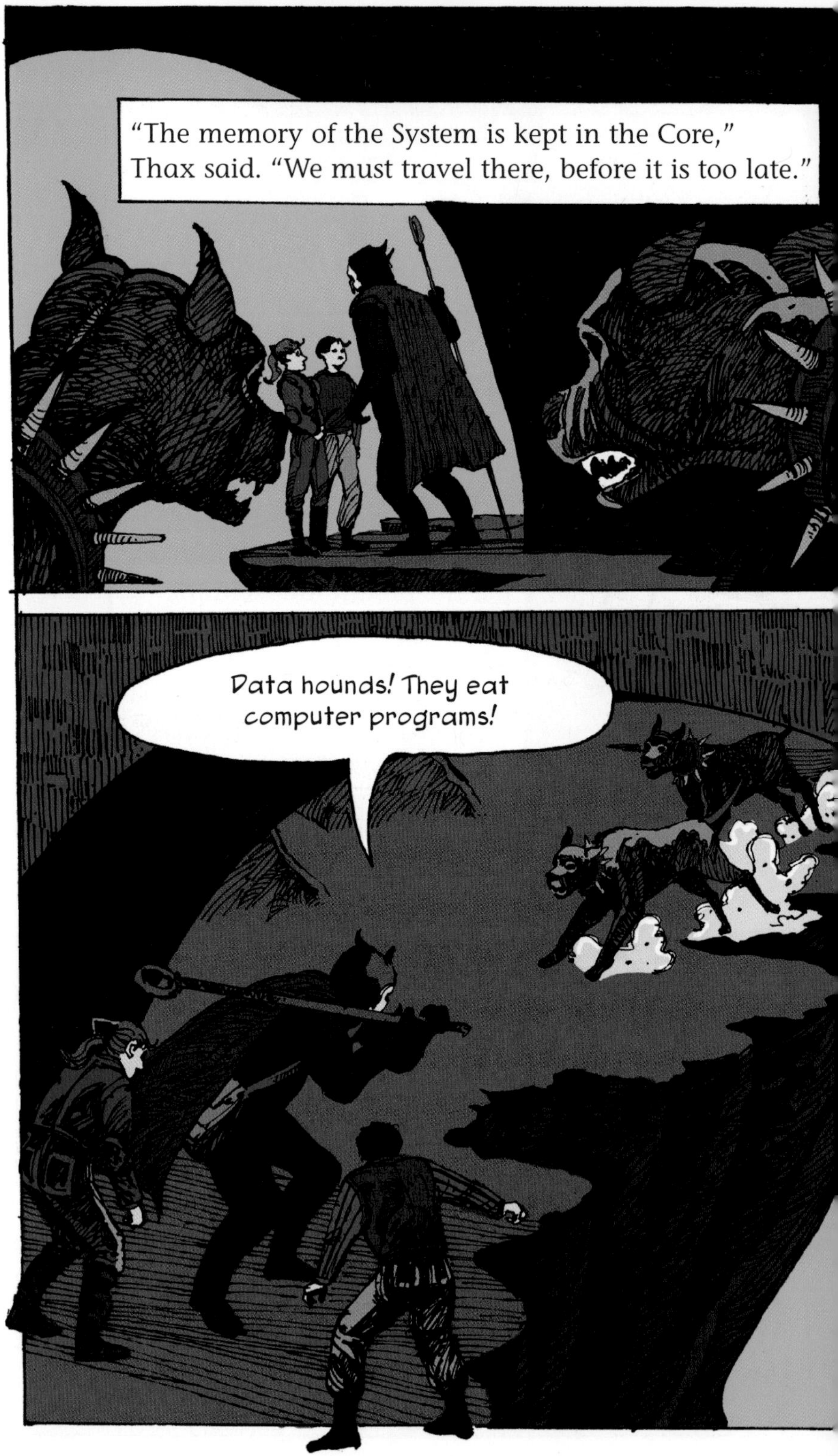
"The memory of the System is kept in the Core," Thax said. "We must travel there, before it is too late."
Data hounds! They eat computer programs!

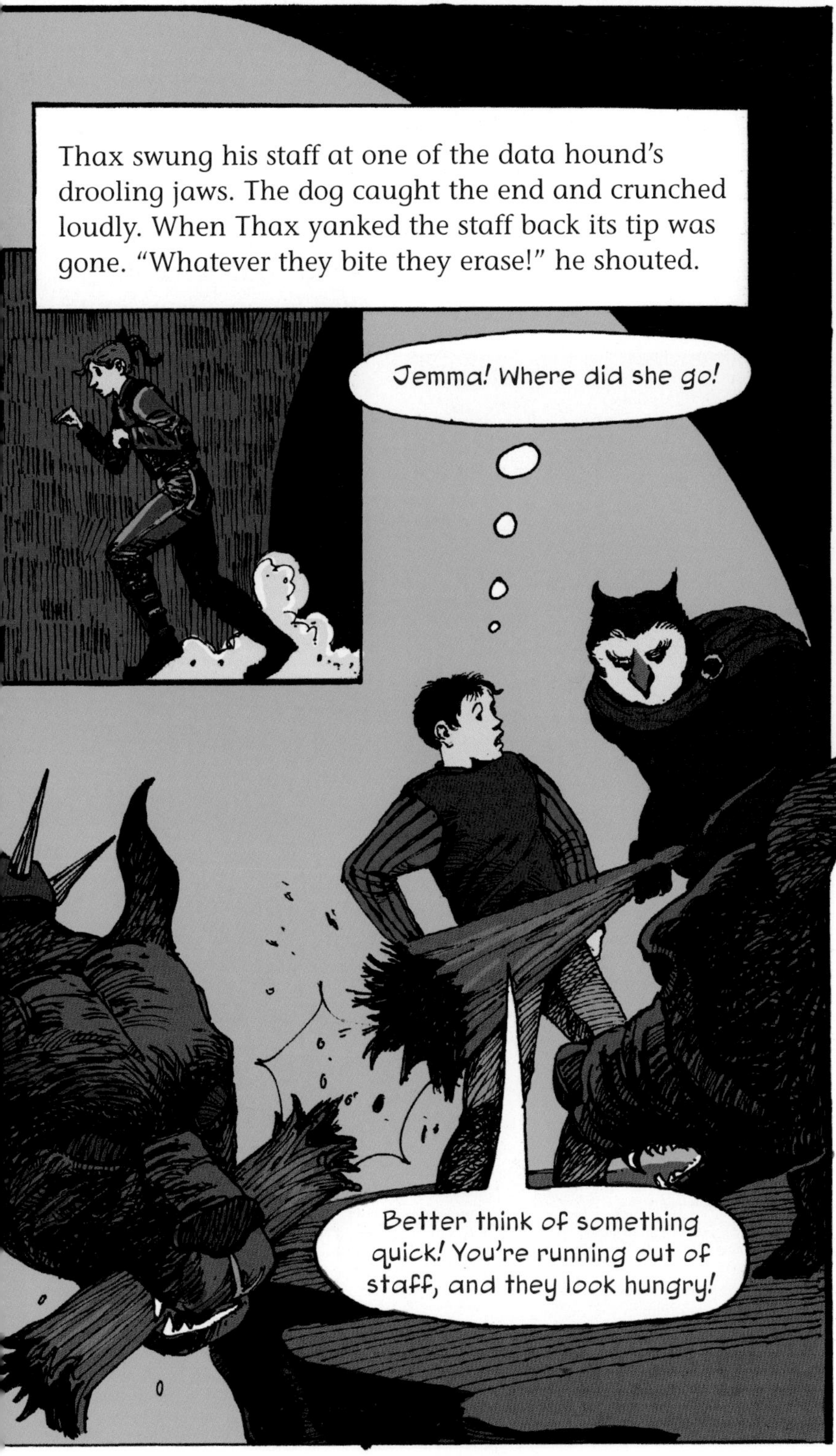
Thax swung his staff at one of the data hound's drooling jaws. The dog caught the end and crunched loudly. When Thax yanked the staff back its tip was gone. "Whatever they bite they erase!" he shouted.
Jemma! Where did she go!
Better think of something quick! You're running out of staff, and they look hungry!

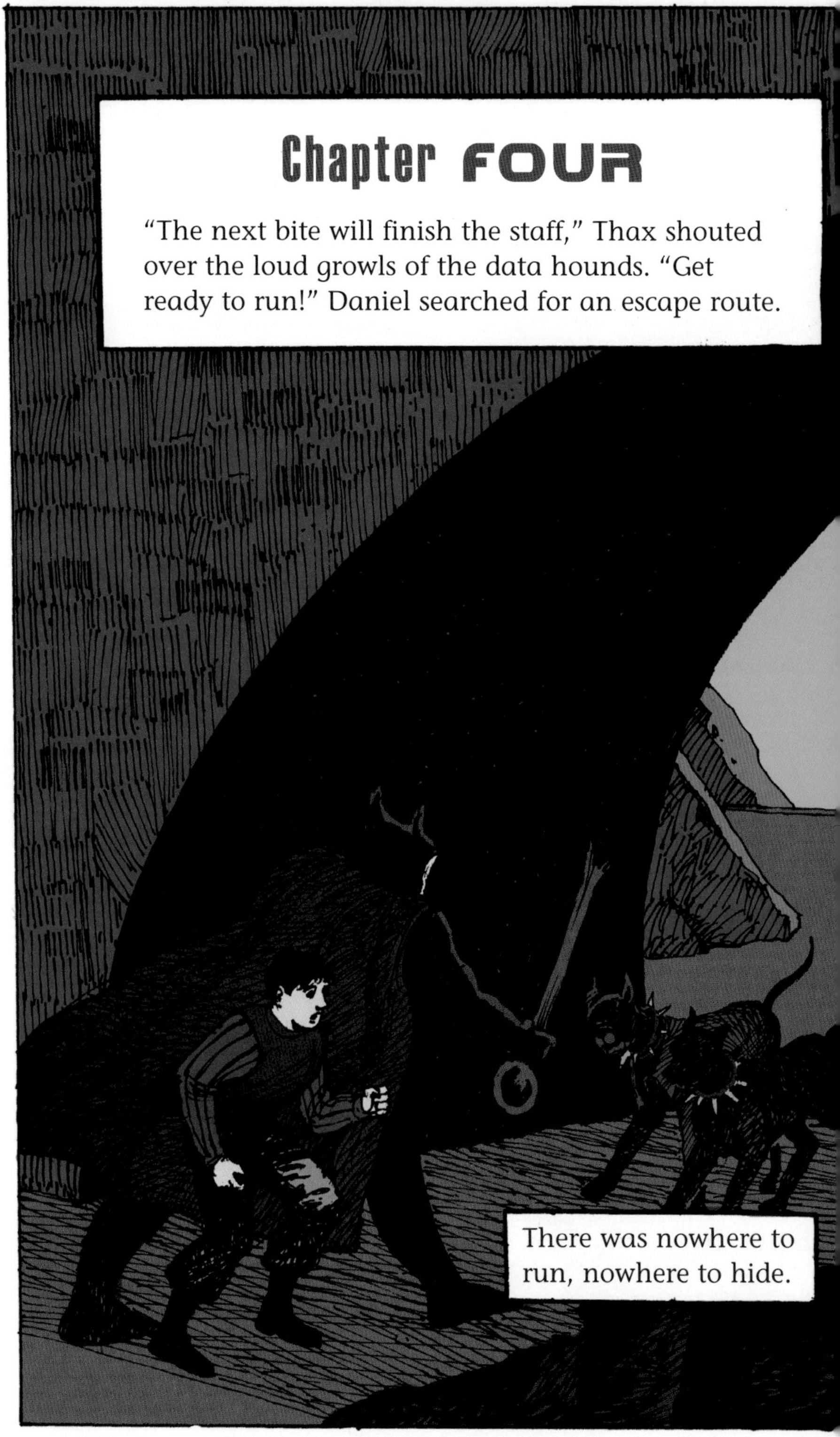
Chapter FOUR
"The next bite will finish the staff," Thax shouted over the loud growls of the data hounds. "Get ready to run!" Daniel searched for an escape route.
There was nowhere to run, nowhere to hide.

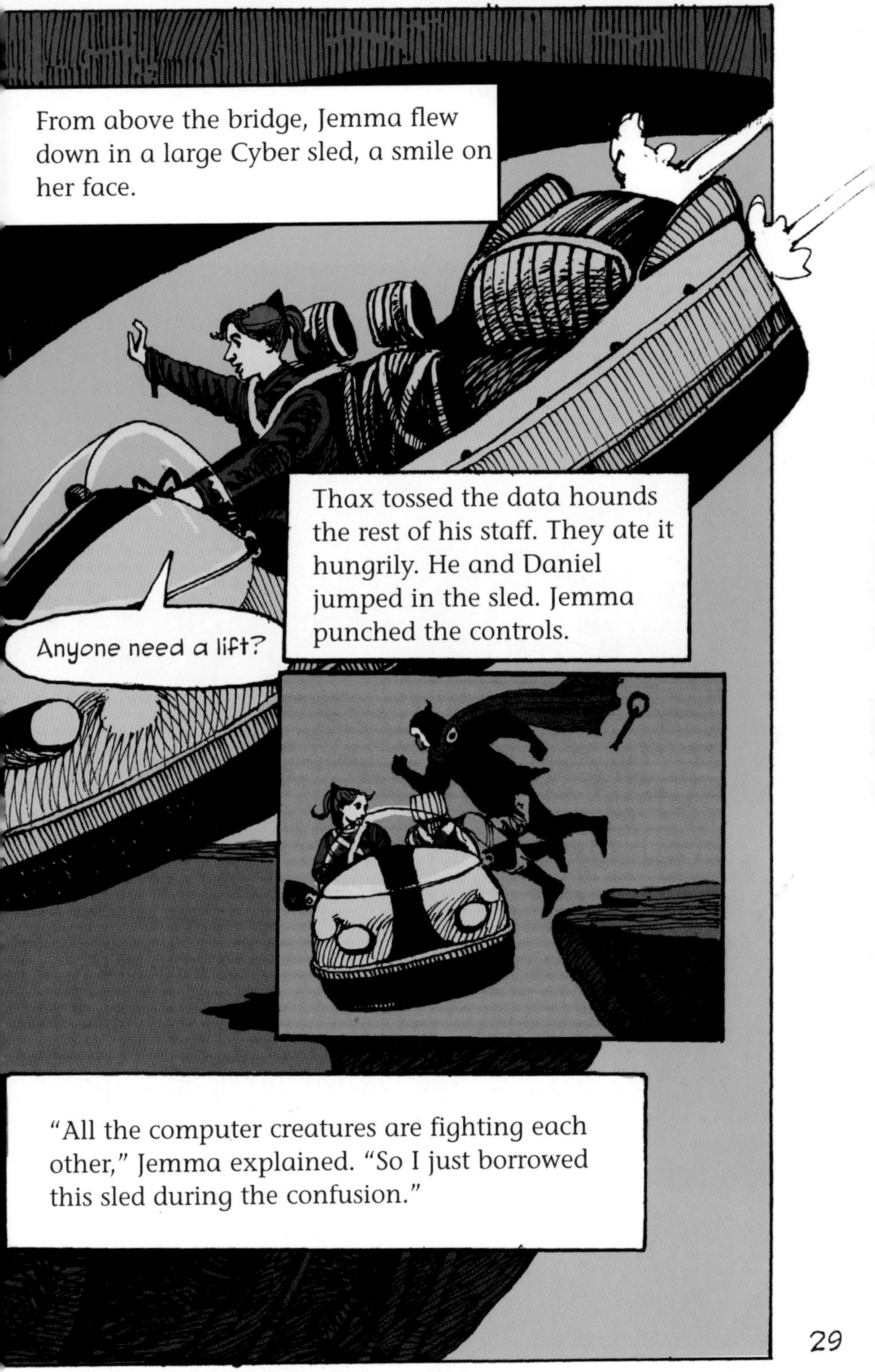
From above the bridge, Jemma flew down in a large Cyber sled, a smile on her face.
Anyone need a lift?
Thax tossed the data hounds the rest of his staff. They ate it hungrily. He and Daniel jumped in the sled. Jemma punched the controls.
"All the computer creatures are fighting each other," Jemma explained. "So I just borrowed this sled during the confusion."

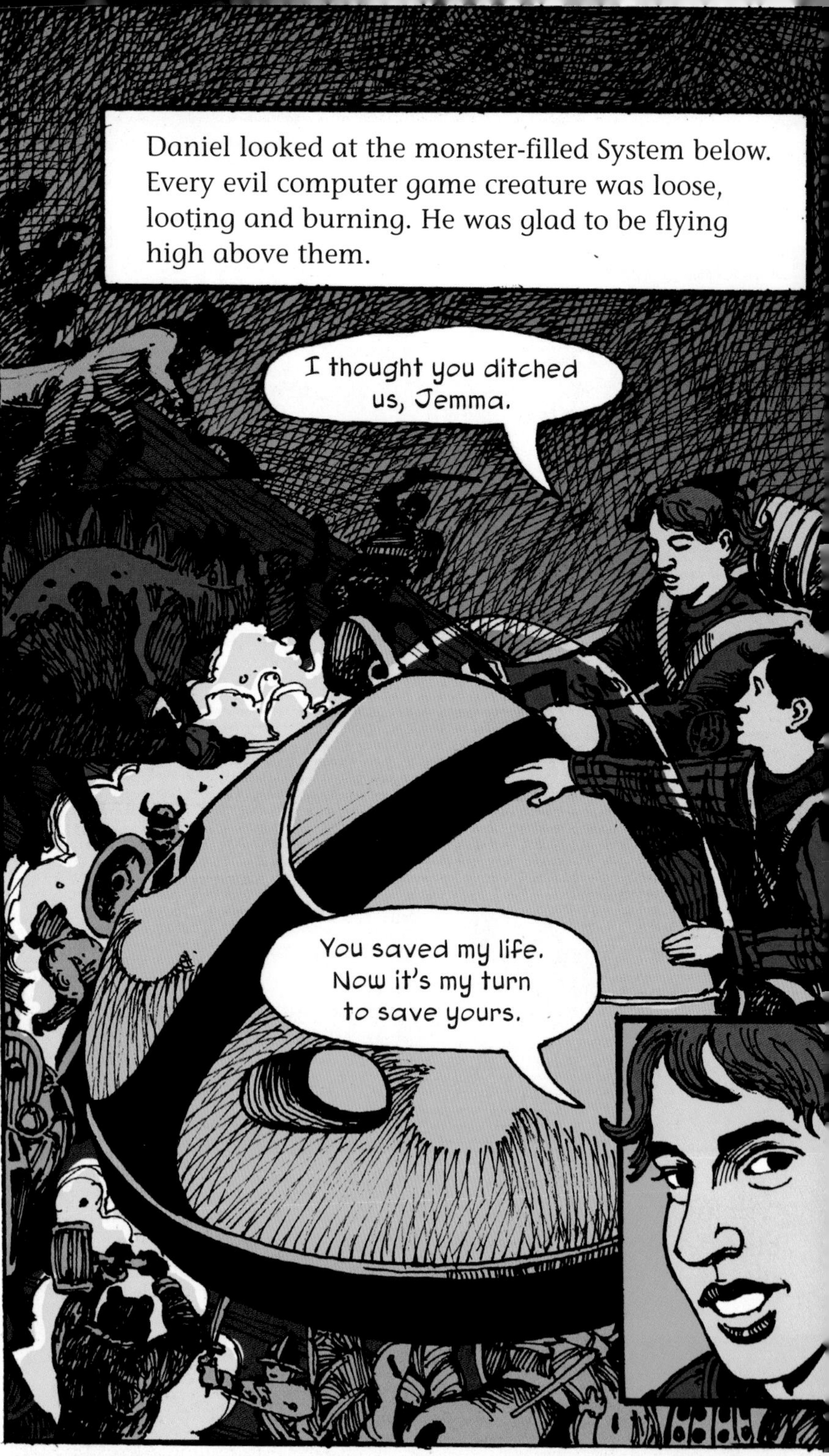
Daniel looked at the monster-filled System below. Every evil computer game creature was loose, looting and burning. He was glad to be flying high above them.
I thought you ditched us, Jemma.
You saved my life. Now it's my turn to save yours.

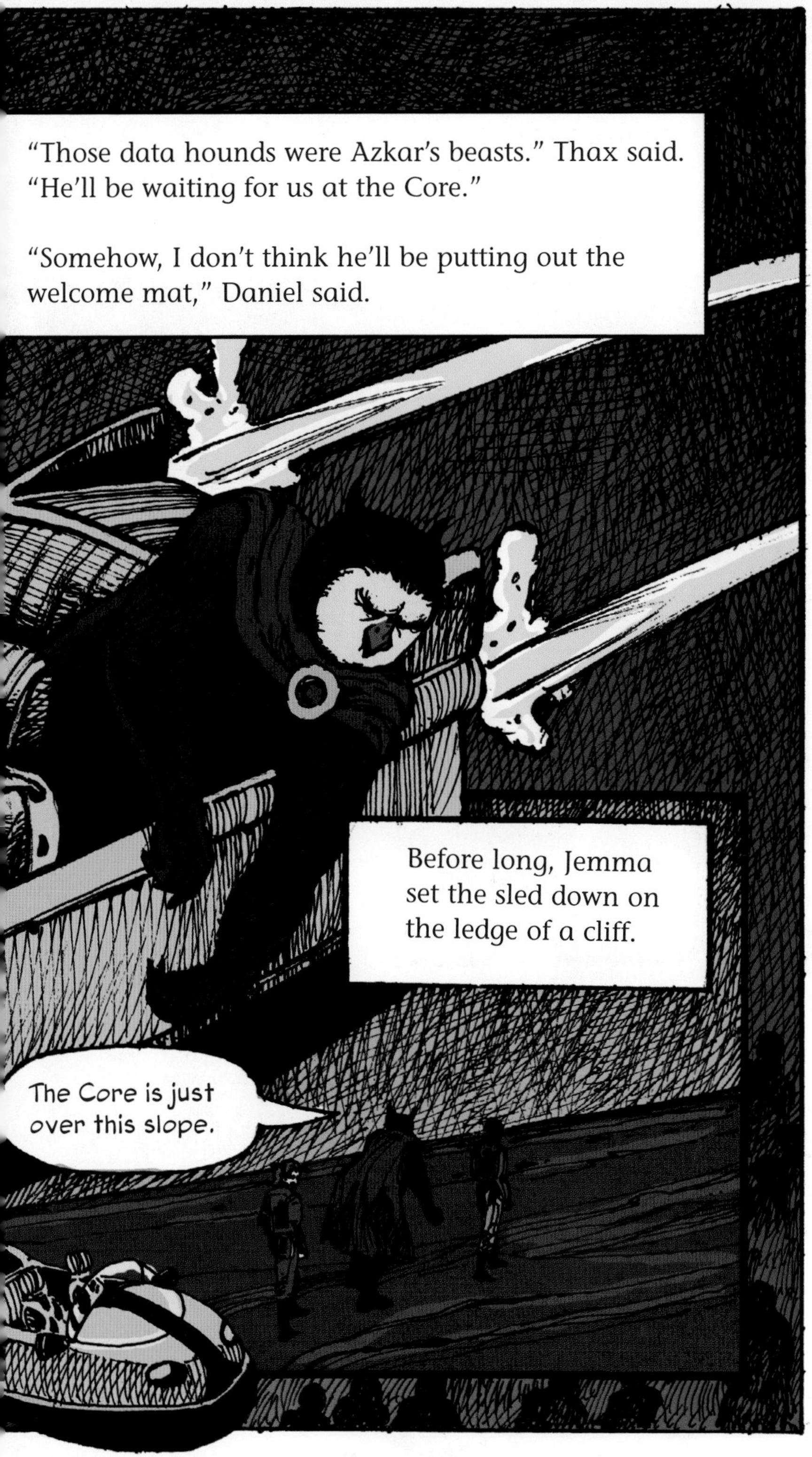
"Those data hounds were Azkar's beasts." Thax said. "He'll be waiting for us at the Core."
"Somehow, I don't think he'll be putting out the welcome mat," Daniel said.
Before long, Jemma set the sled down on the ledge of a cliff.
The Core is just over this slope.

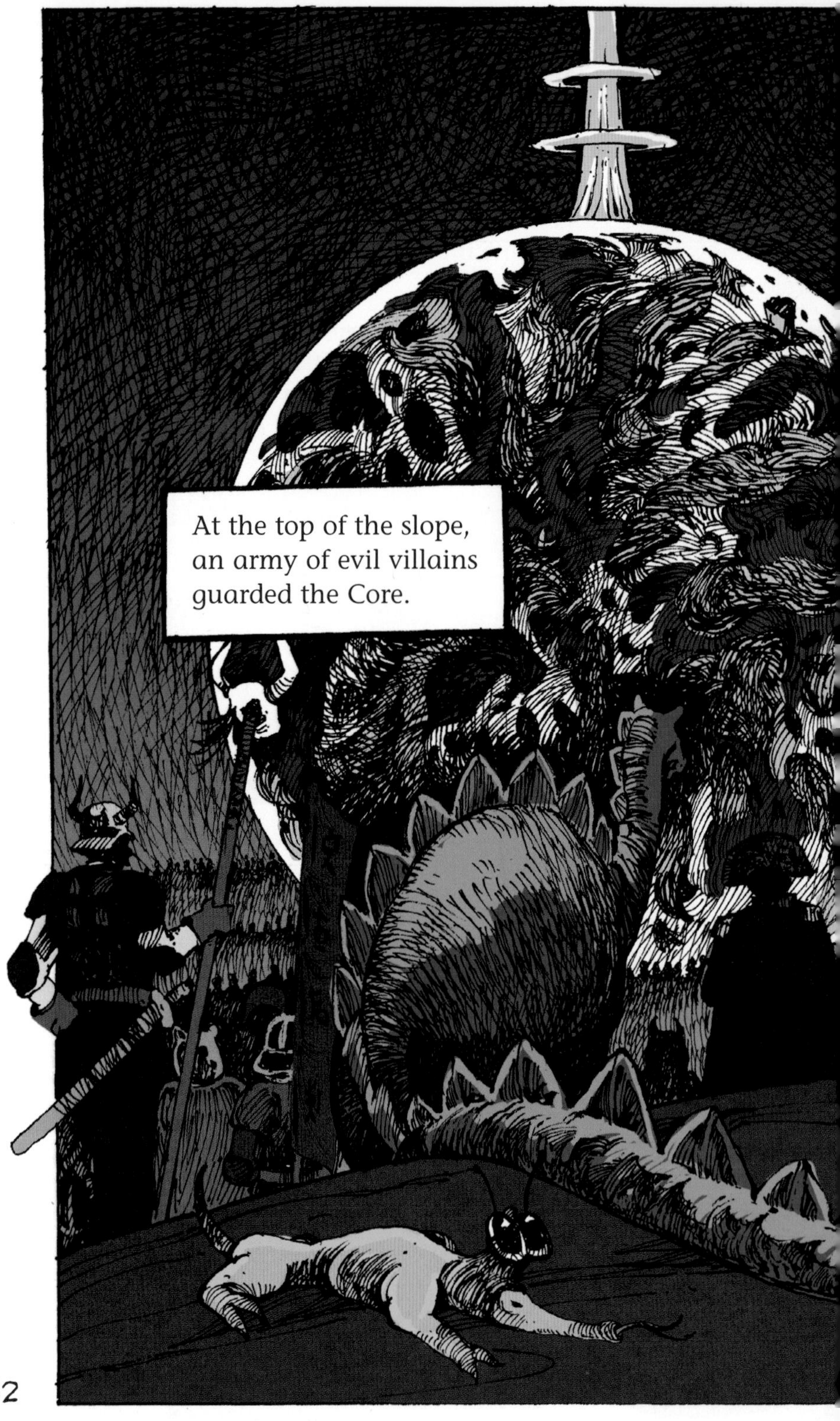
At the top of the slope, an army of evil villains guarded the Core.

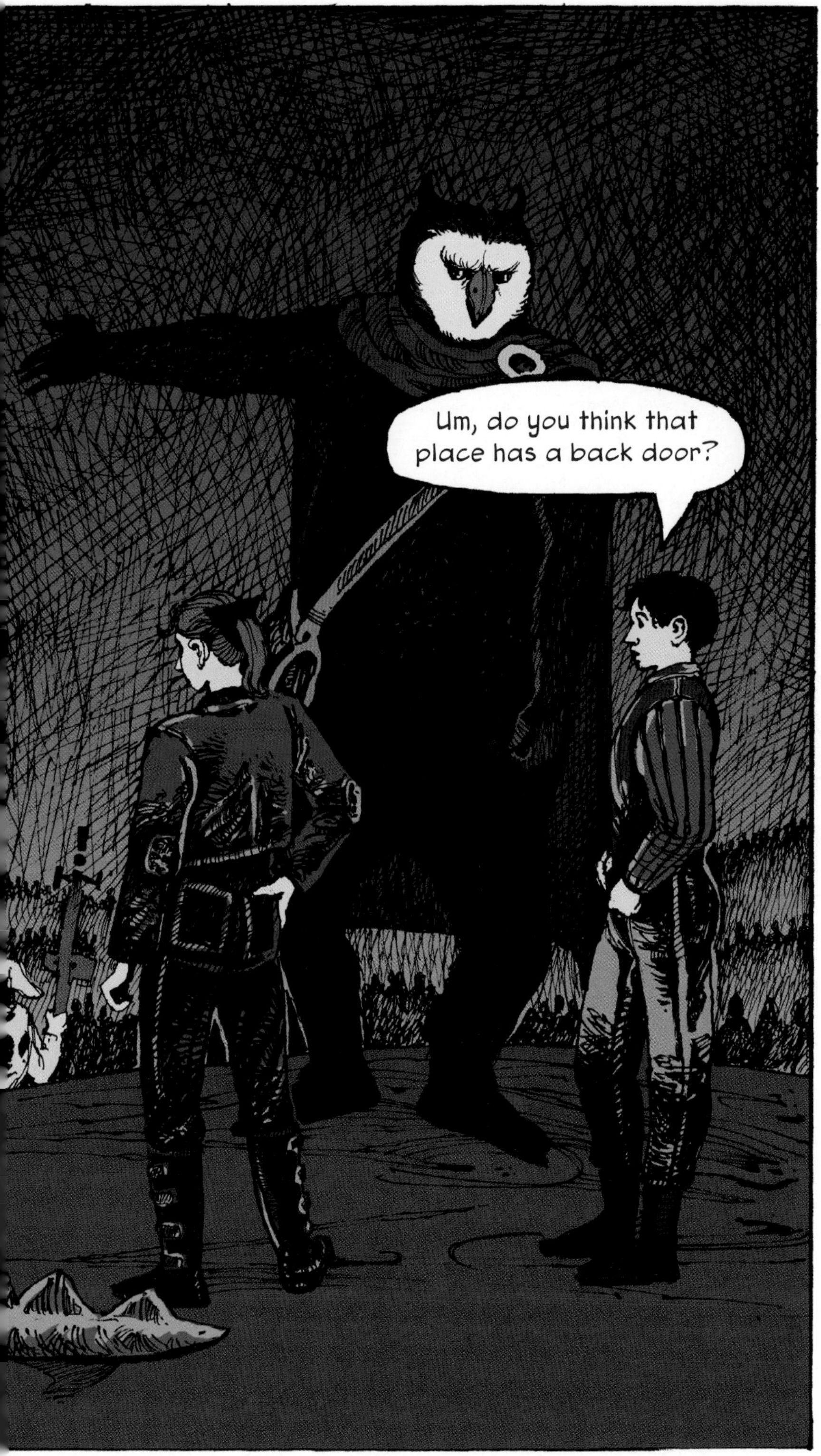
Um, do you think that place has a back door?

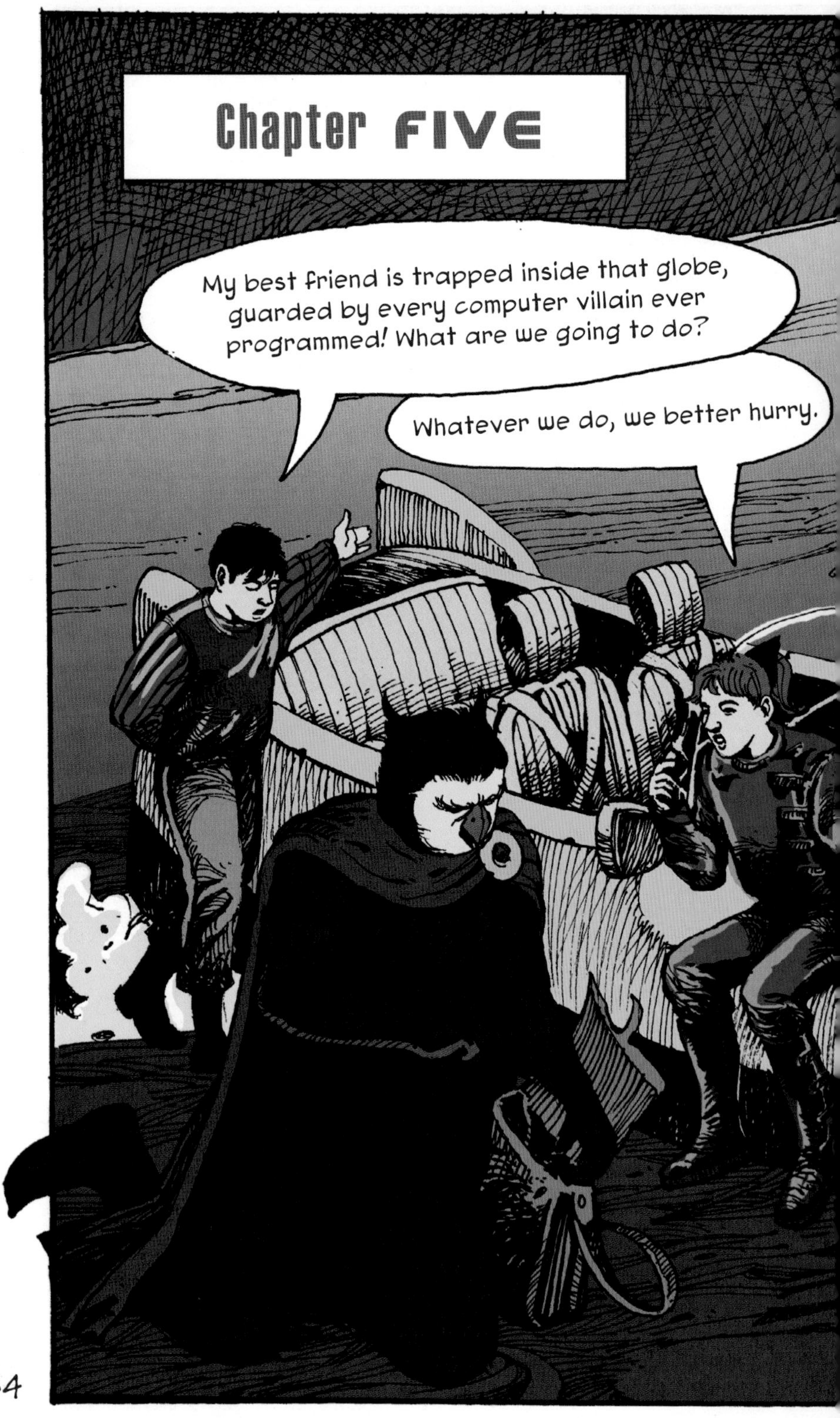
Chapter FIVE
My best friend is trapped inside that globe, guarded by every computer villain ever programmed! What are we going to do?
Whatever we do, we better hurry.

"What?" exclaimed Daniel, looking at Jemma's timer. "There must be more time than that."

"Time inside the System moves differently than in the real world," Jemma explained. "When this timer reaches zero, we're in big trouble!"

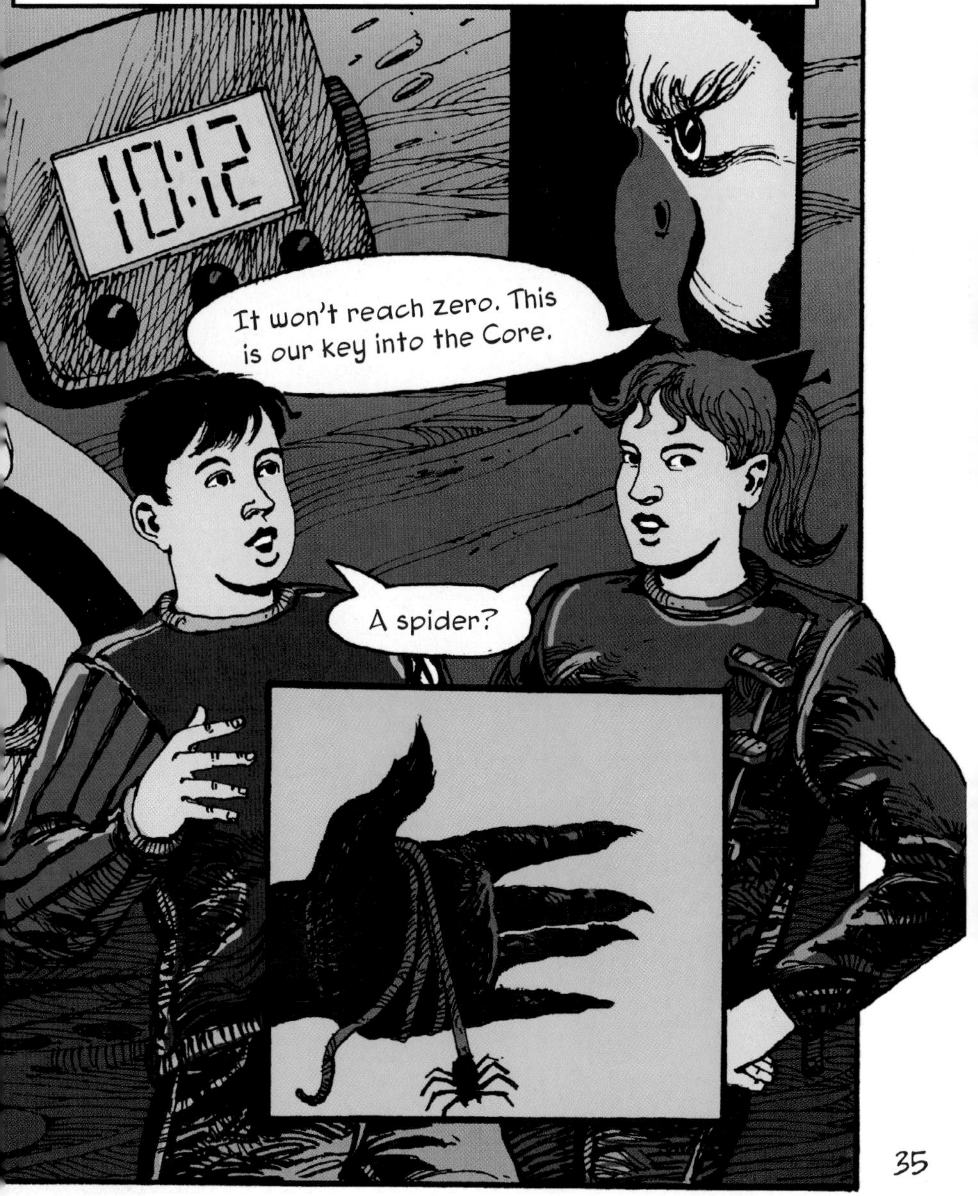
10:12
It won't reach zero. This is our key into the Core.
A spider?

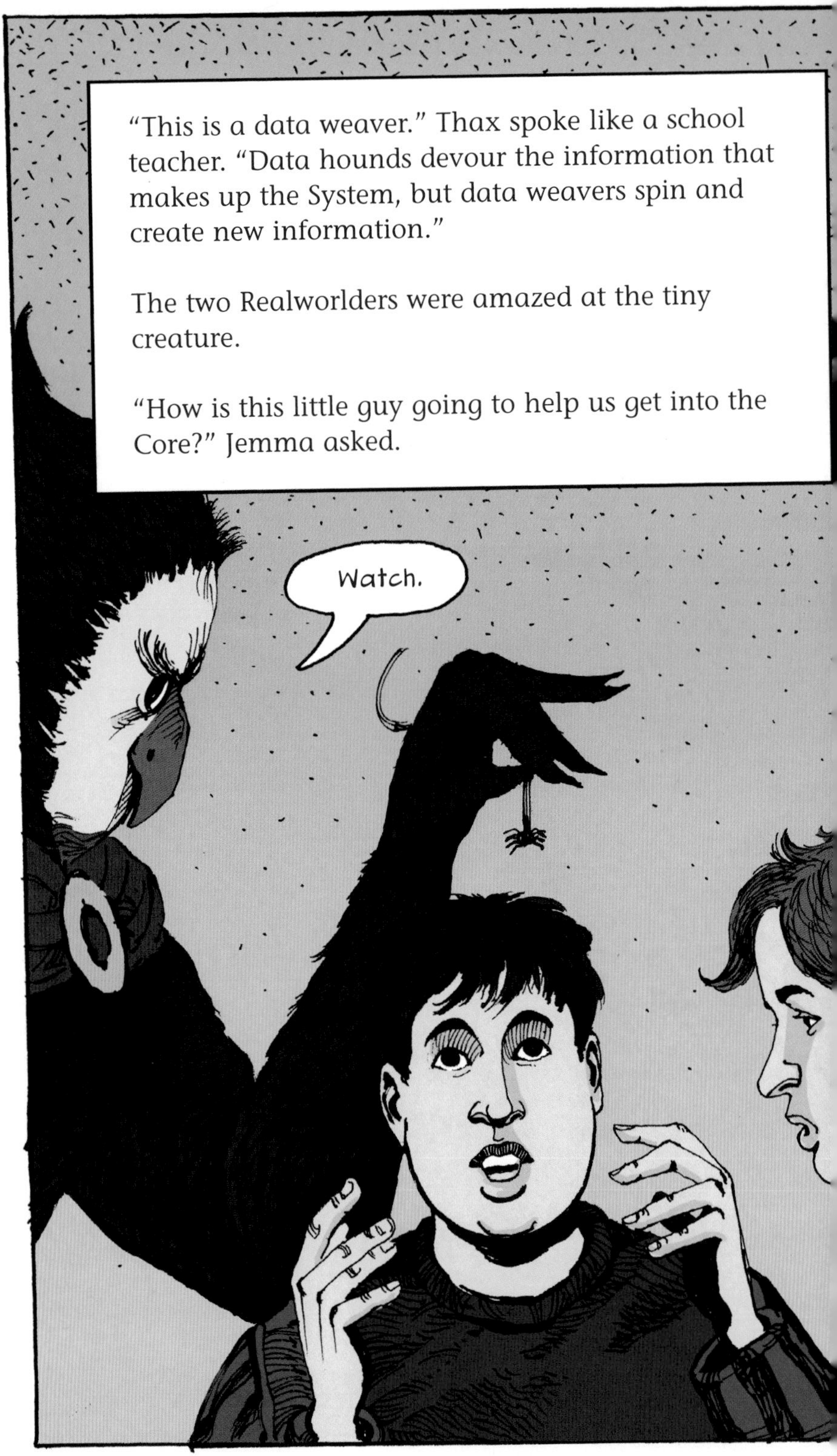
"This is a data weaver." Thax spoke like a school teacher. "Data hounds devour the information that makes up the System, but data weavers spin and create new information."
The two Realworlders were amazed at the tiny creature.
"How is this little guy going to help us get into the Core?" Jemma asked.
Watch.

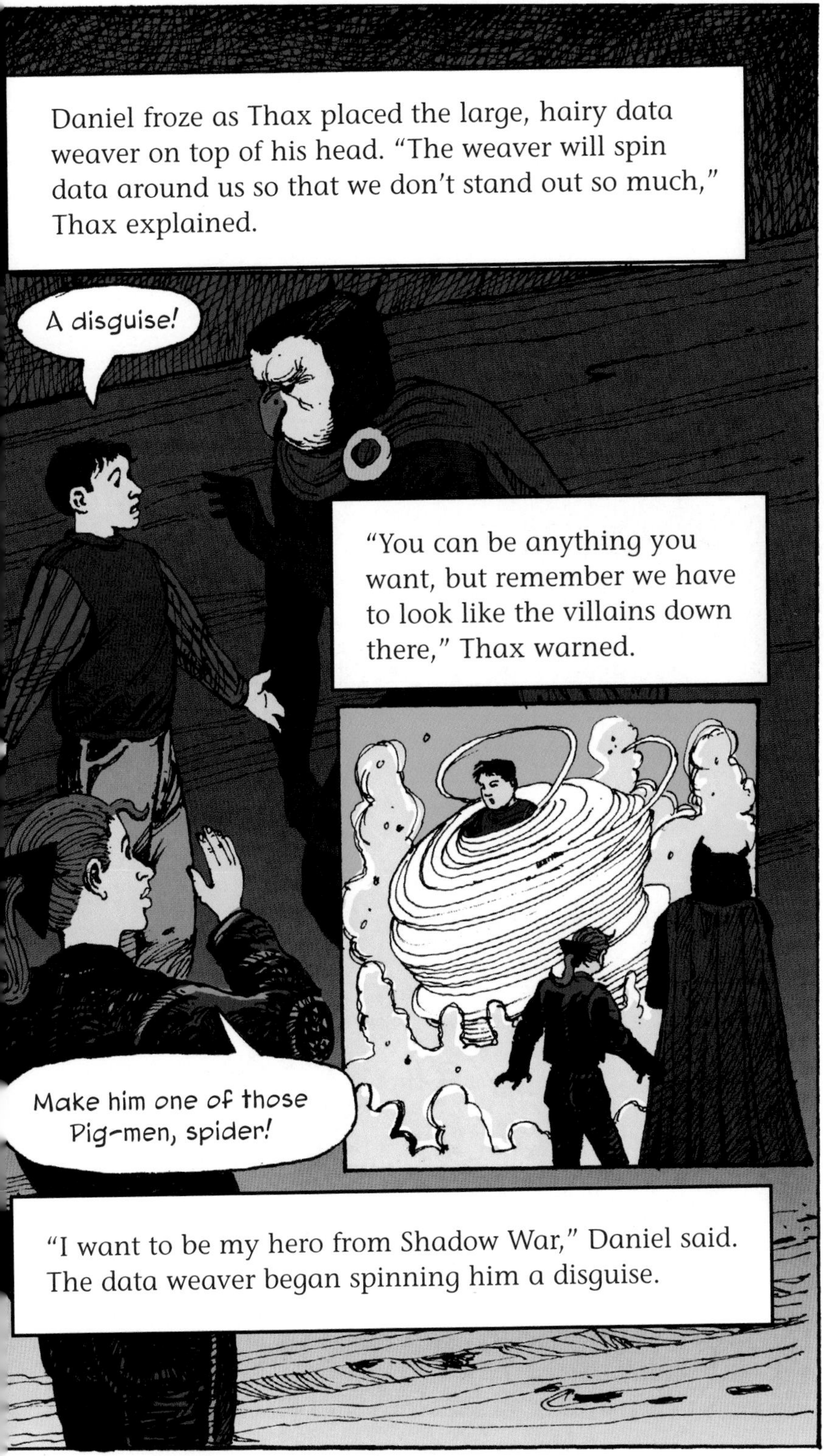
Daniel froze as Thax placed the large, hairy data weaver on top of his head. "The weaver will spin data around us so that we don't stand out so much," Thax explained.
A disguise!
"You can be anything you want, but remember we have to look like the villains down there," Thax warned.
Make him one of those Pig-men, spider!
"I want to be my hero from Shadow War," Daniel said. The data weaver began spinning him a disguise.

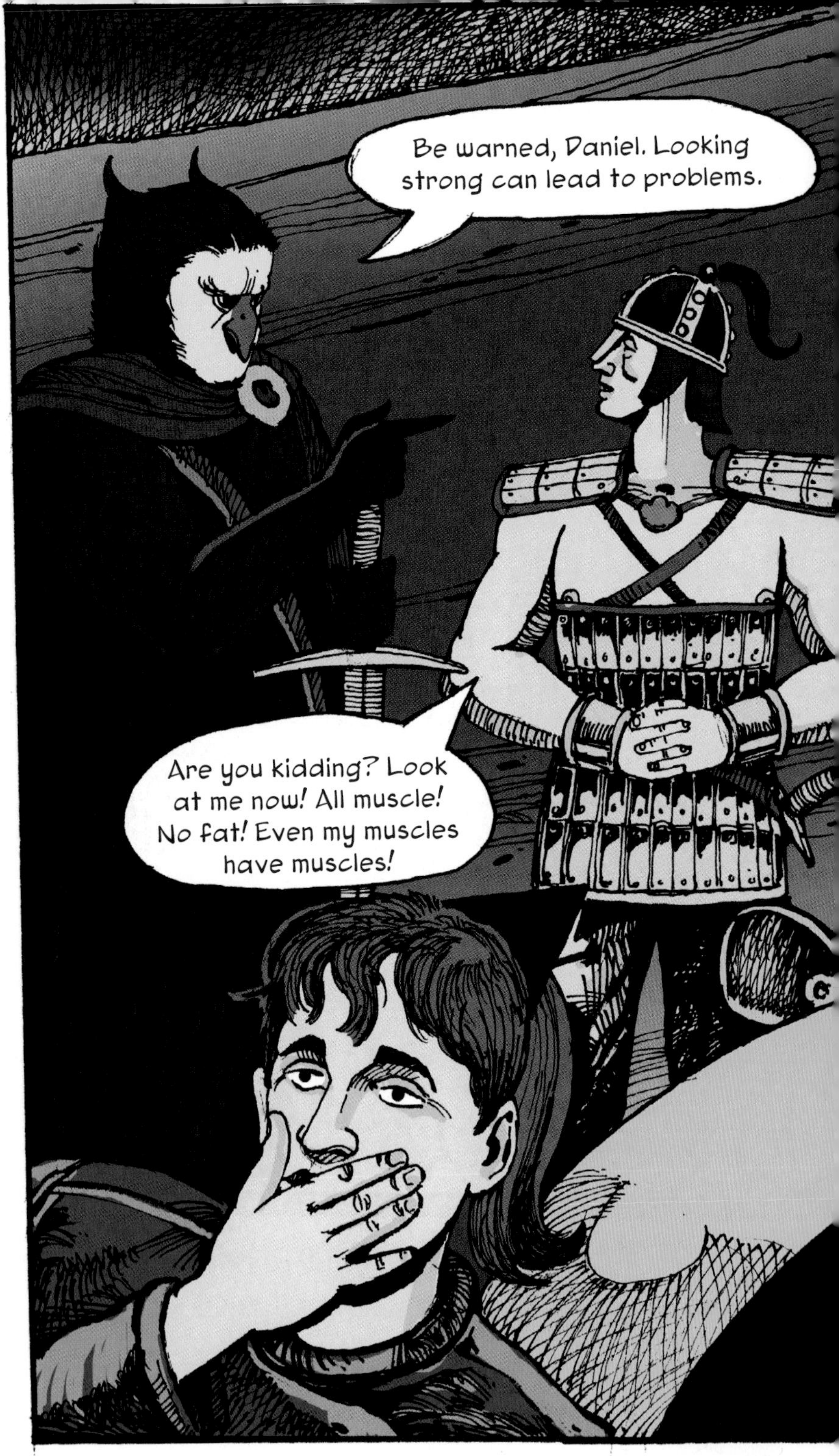
Be warned, Daniel. Looking strong can lead to problems.
Are you kidding? Look at me now! All muscle! No fat! Even my muscles have muscles!

The data weaver spun another disguise around Jemma. "That's more like it," she said. With its work done, the spider slipped into Thax's bag. They were ready to struggle through the sea of computer villains.

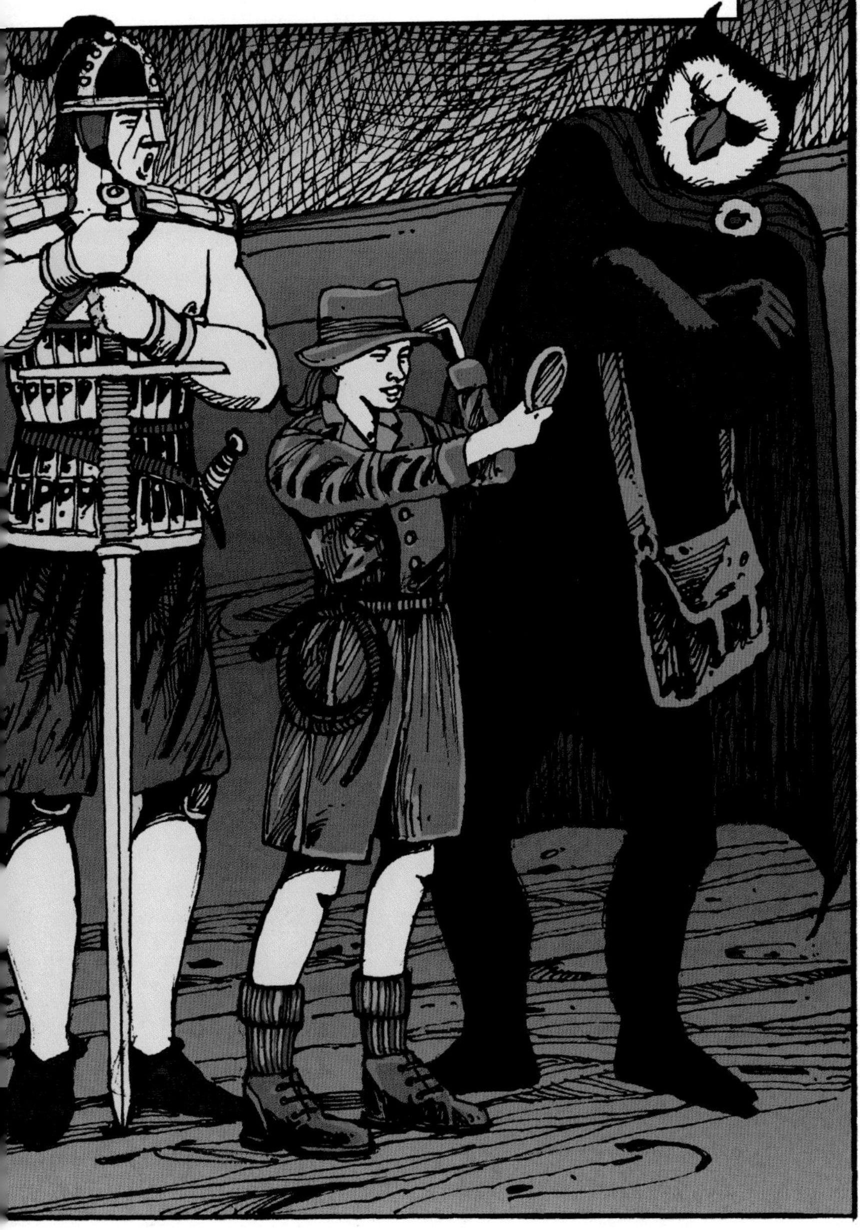

Chapter SIX

The army of evil monsters had set up outside the Core. Thax, Daniel, and Jemma abandoned their sled when the crowds got too thick. Soon they were walking down a narrow street that led to the giant Core. This was no place for polite manners. Pushing and shoving was the only way to move ahead.

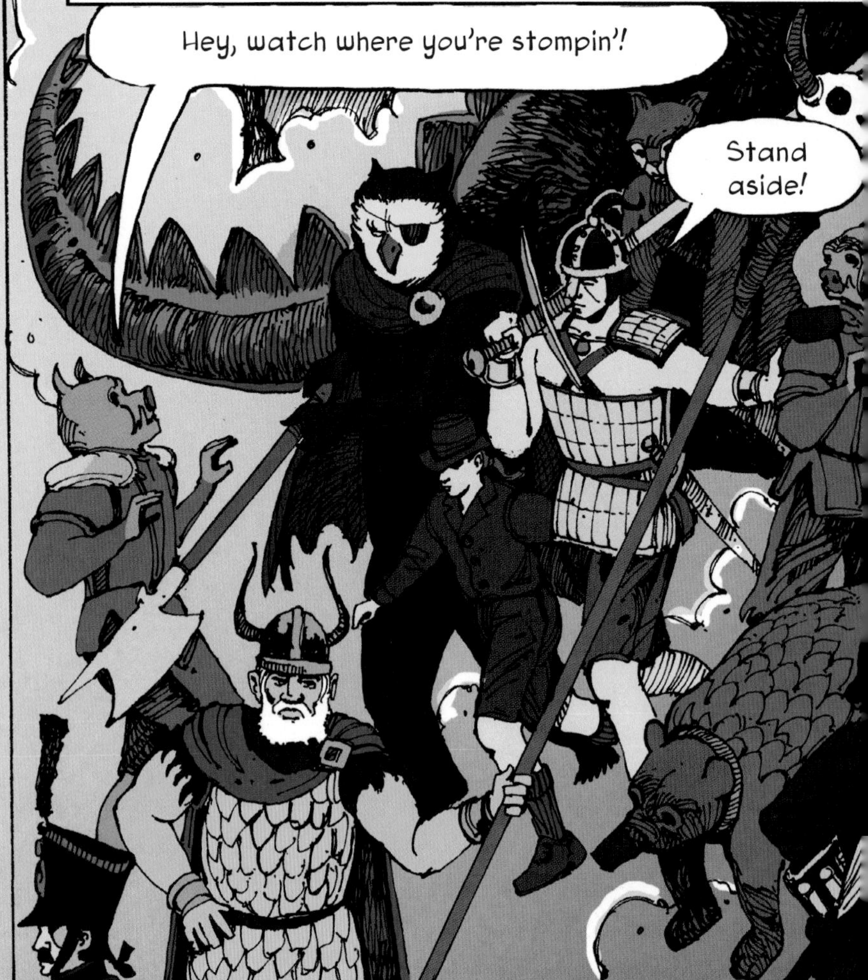
Hey, watch where you're stompin'!
Stand aside!

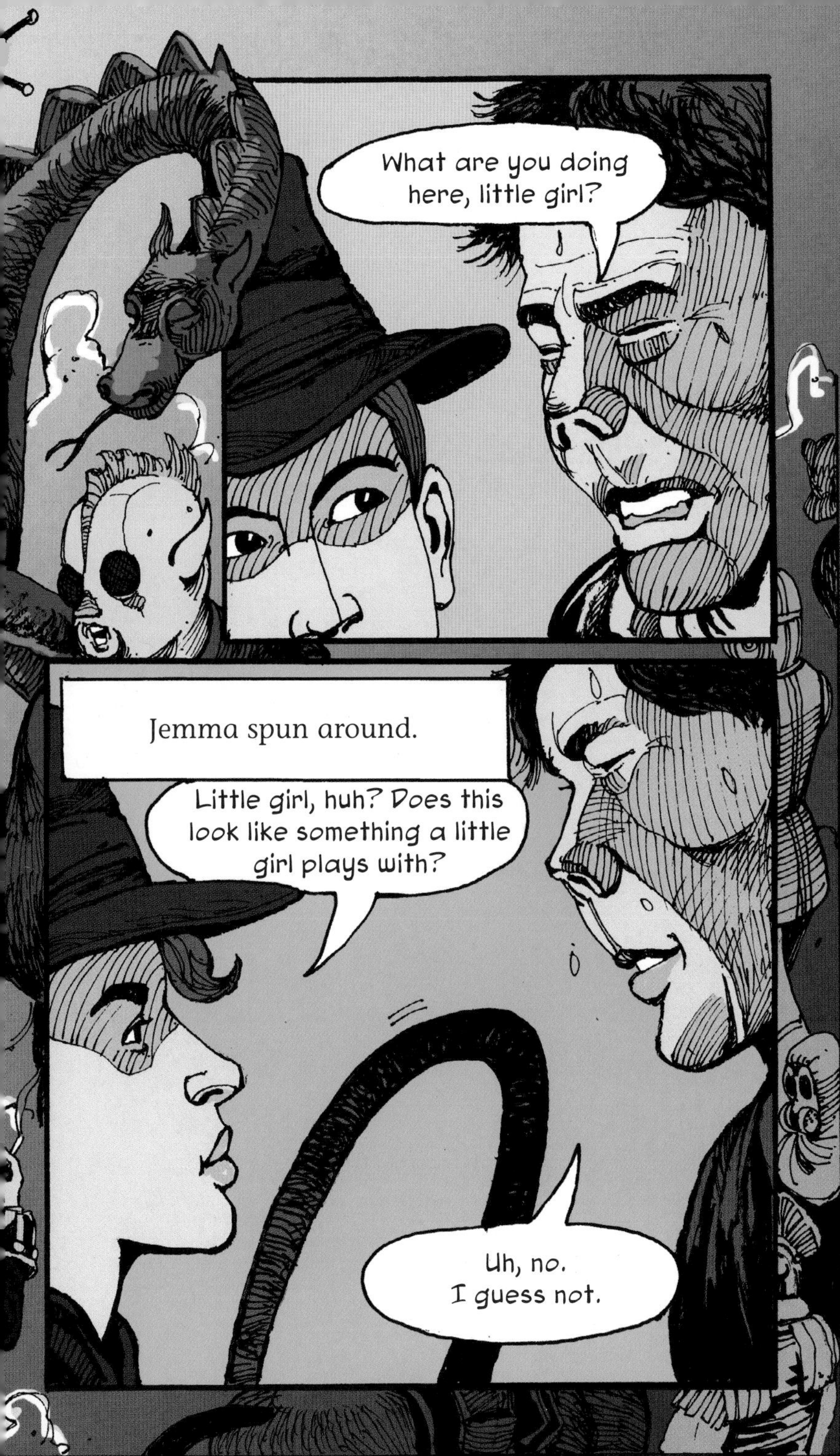
What are you doing here, little girl?
Jemma spun around.
Little girl, huh? Does this look like something a little girl plays with?
Uh, no. I guess not.

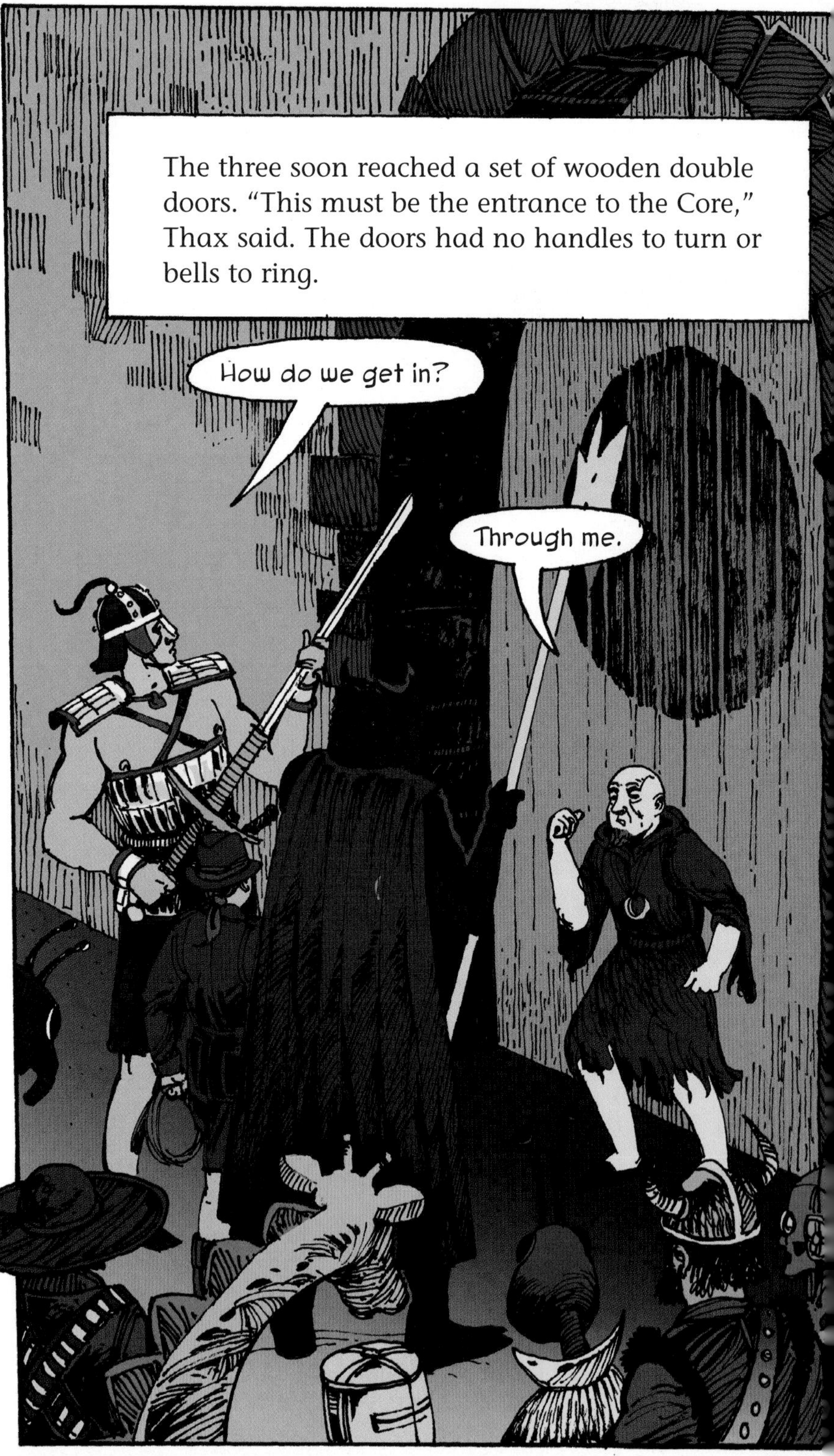
The three soon reached a set of wooden double doors. “This must be the entrance to the Core,” Thax said. The doors had no handles to turn or bells to ring.
How do we get in?
Through me.

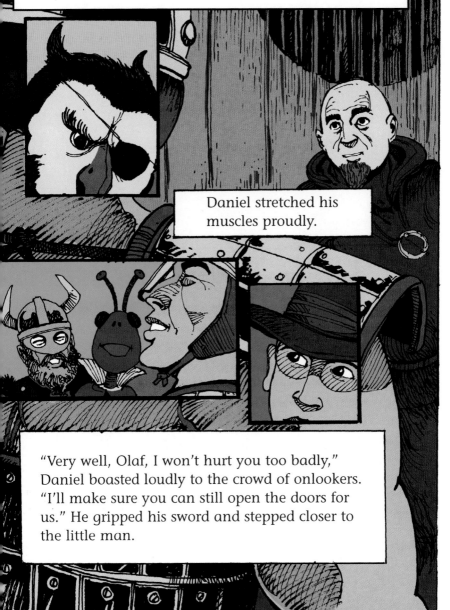

"I am Olaf, the Gatekeeper," the tiny man said with pride. "To get through those doors you must defeat me in combat."

Daniel stretched his muscles proudly.

"Very well, Olaf, I won't hurt you too badly," Daniel boasted loudly to the crowd of onlookers. "I'll make sure you can still open the doors for us." He gripped his sword and stepped closer to the little man.

43

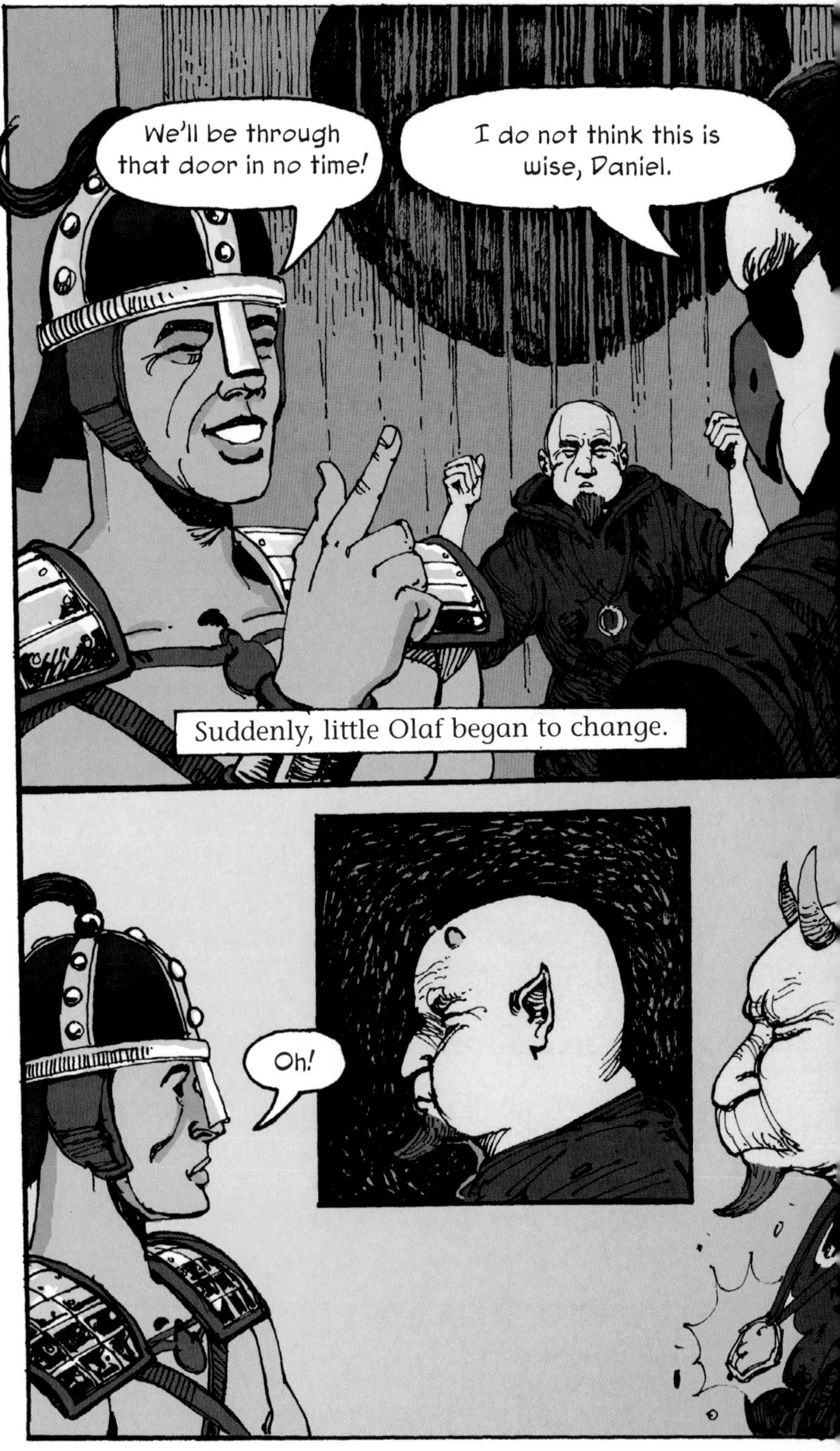
We'll be through that door in no time!
I do not think this is wise, Daniel.
Suddenly, little Olaf began to change.
Oh!

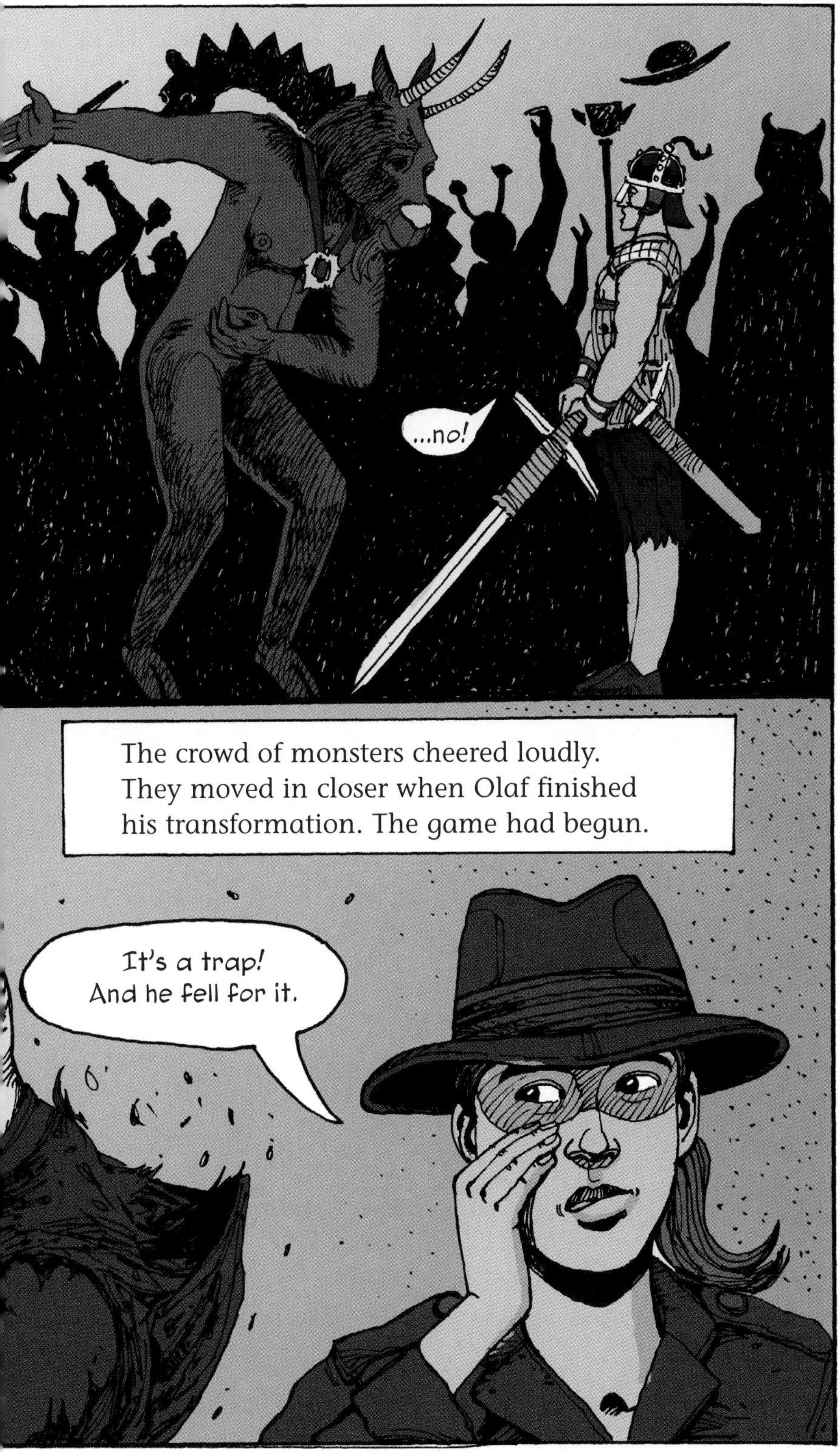
...no!
The crowd of monsters cheered loudly. They moved in closer when Olaf finished his transformation. The game had begun.
It's a trap! And he fell for it.

Chapter SEVEN

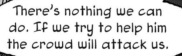

There's nothing we can do. If we try to help him the crowd will attack us.

Daniel, alone, had to defeat the beast to get into the Core. He quickly dodged Olaf's claw. One hit with those razor-sharp blades and he'd be finished. He soon realized he was no match for the monster, muscles or no muscles.

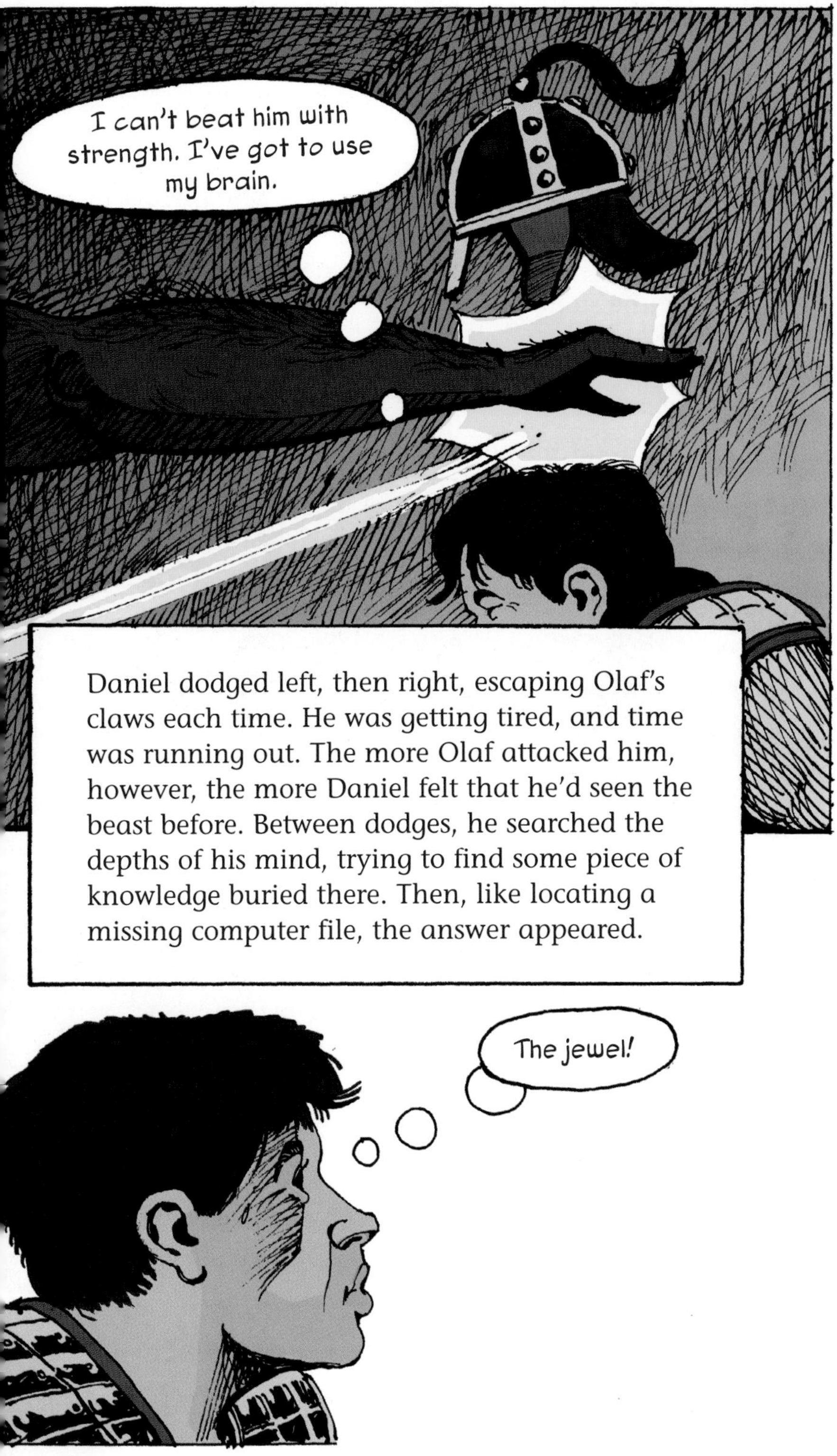
I can't beat him with strength. I've got to use my brain.
Daniel dodged left, then right, escaping Olaf's claws each time. He was getting tired, and time was running out. The more Olaf attacked him, however, the more Daniel felt that he'd seen the beast before. Between dodges, he searched the depths of his mind, trying to find some piece of knowledge buried there. Then, like locating a missing computer file, the answer appeared.
The jewel!

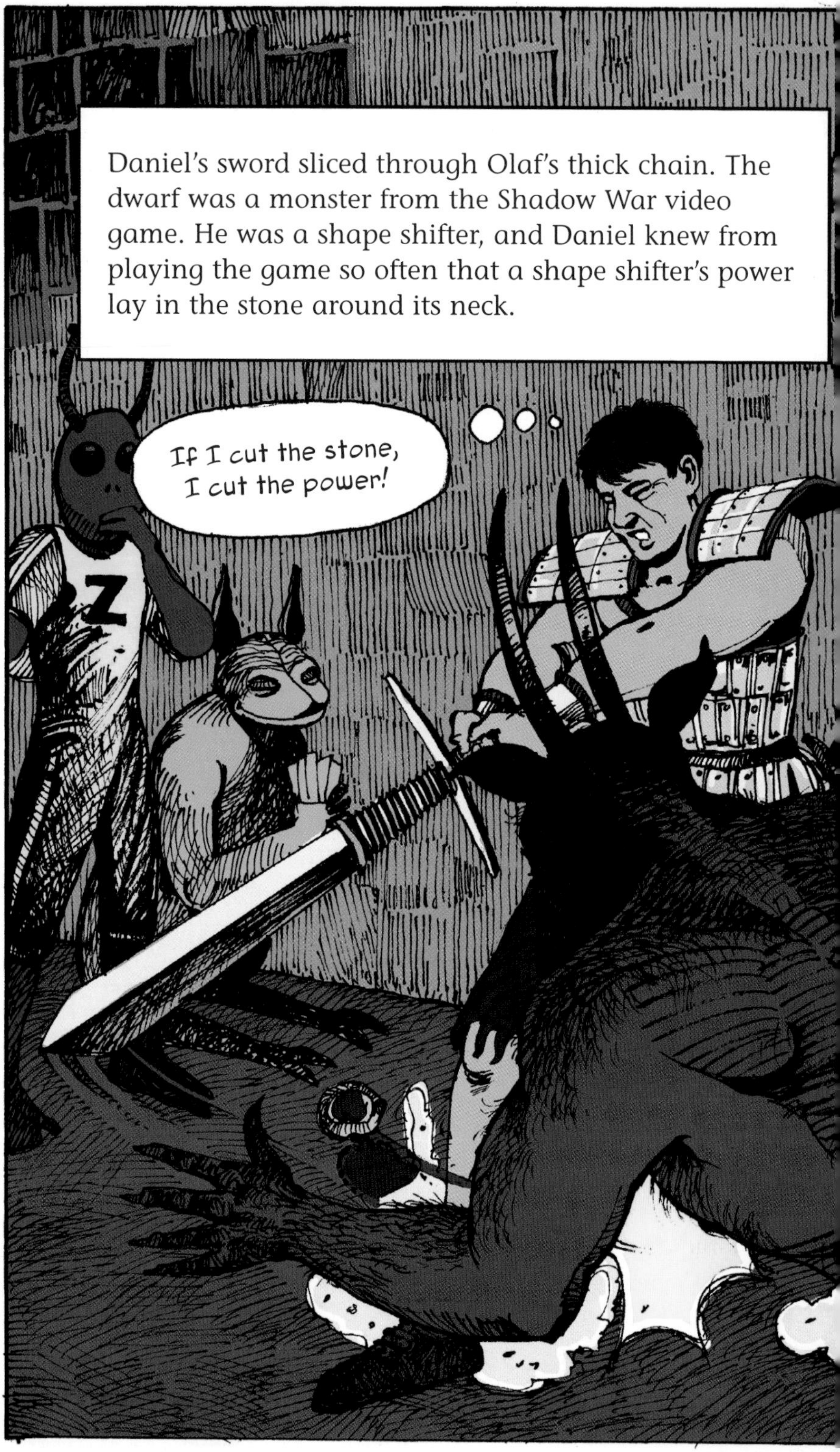
Daniel's sword sliced through Olaf's thick chain. The dwarf was a monster from the Shadow War video game. He was a shape shifter, and Daniel knew from playing the game so often that a shape shifter's power lay in the stone around its neck.
If I cut the stone, I cut the power!

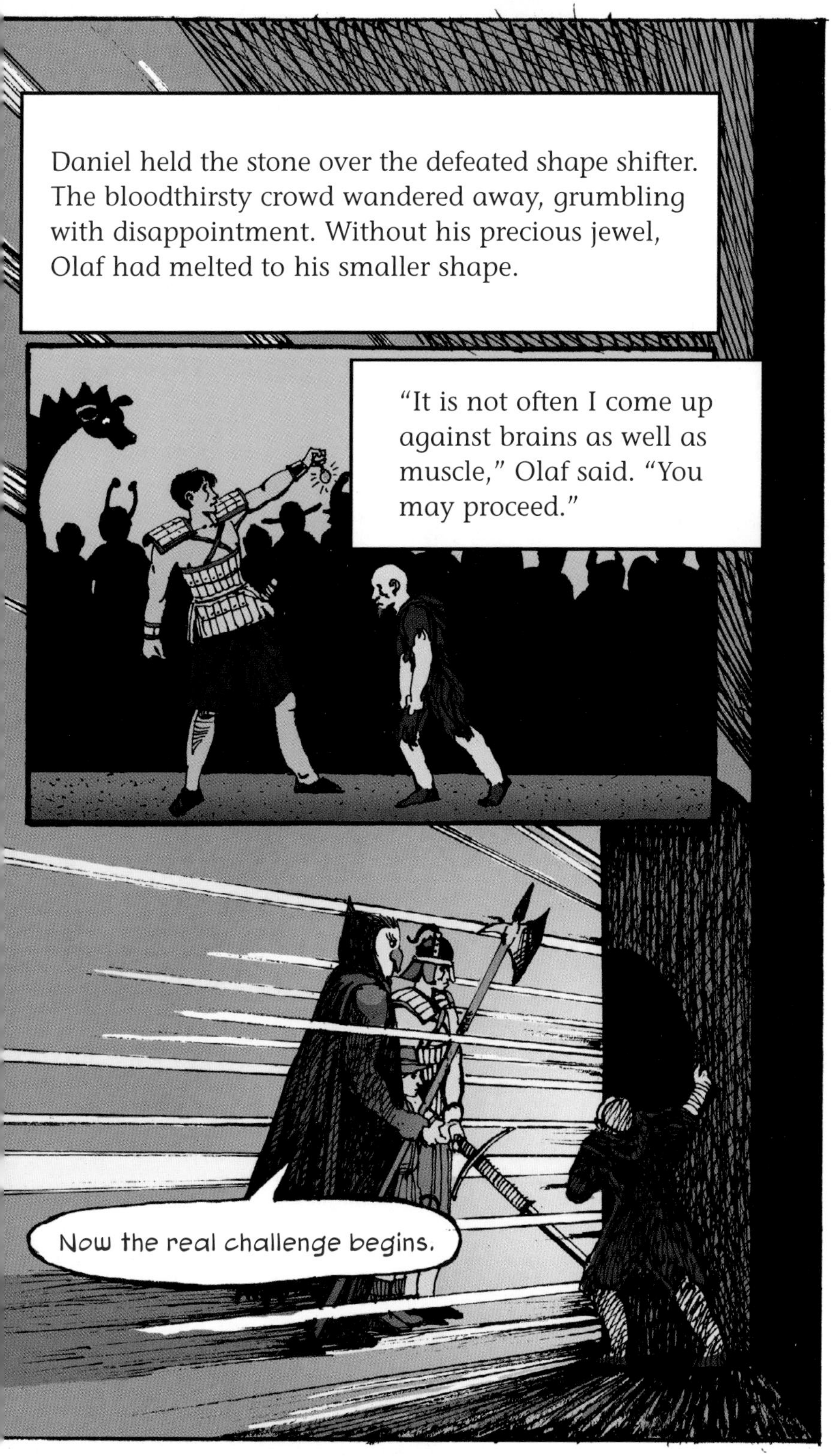
Daniel held the stone over the defeated shape shifter. The bloodthirsty crowd wandered away, grumbling with disappointment. Without his precious jewel, Olaf had melted to his smaller shape.
"It is not often I come up against brains as well as muscle," Olaf said. "You may proceed."
Now the real challenge begins.

Chapter EIGHT

Inside, the Core was pitch black. Thax created a ball of light to guide them. “This place looks like some ancient tomb,” Thax whispered. His voice echoed off the stone walls.

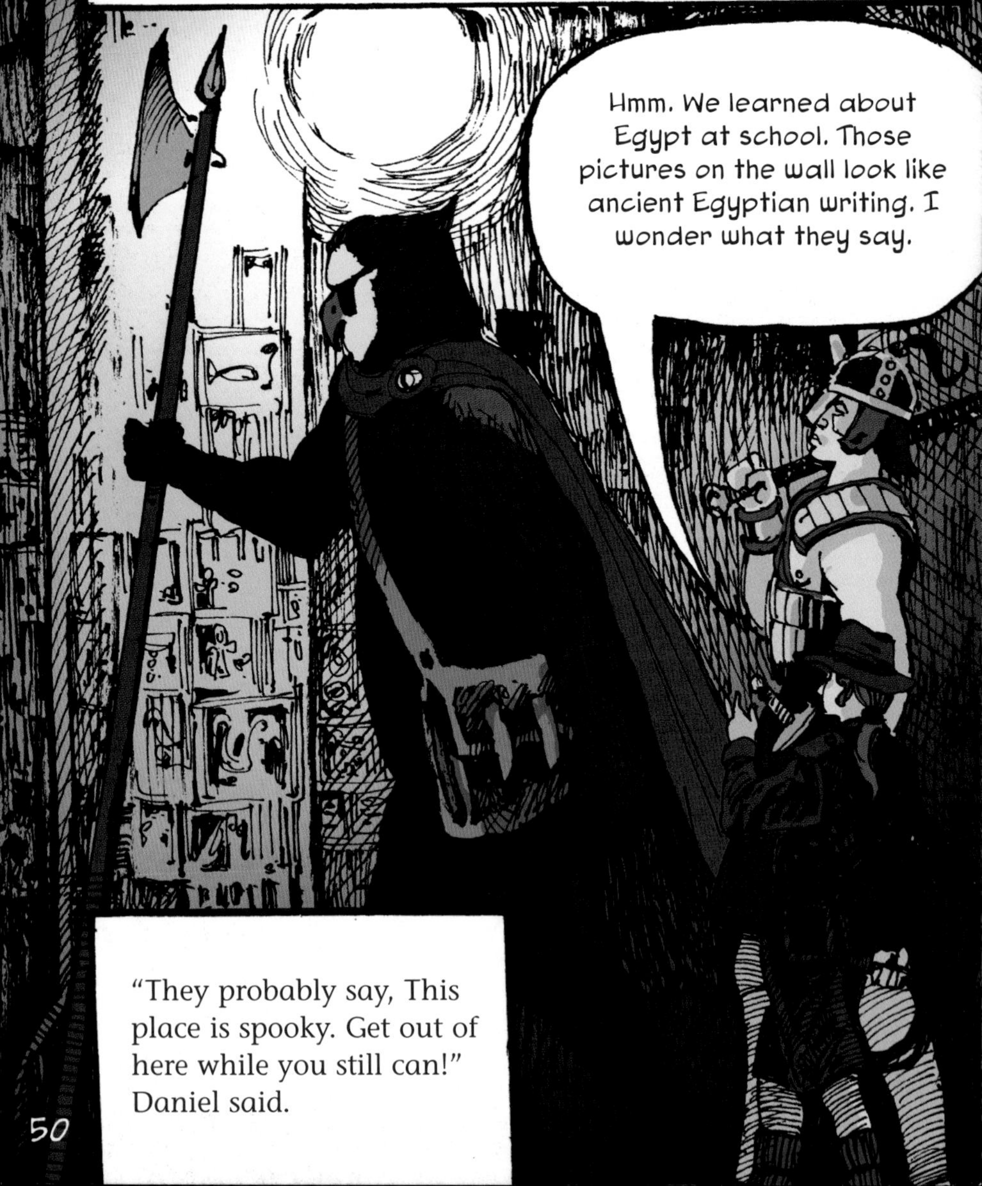
Hmm. We learned about Egypt at school. Those pictures on the wall look like ancient Egyptian writing. I wonder what they say.
“They probably say, This place is spooky. Get out of here while you still can!” Daniel said.

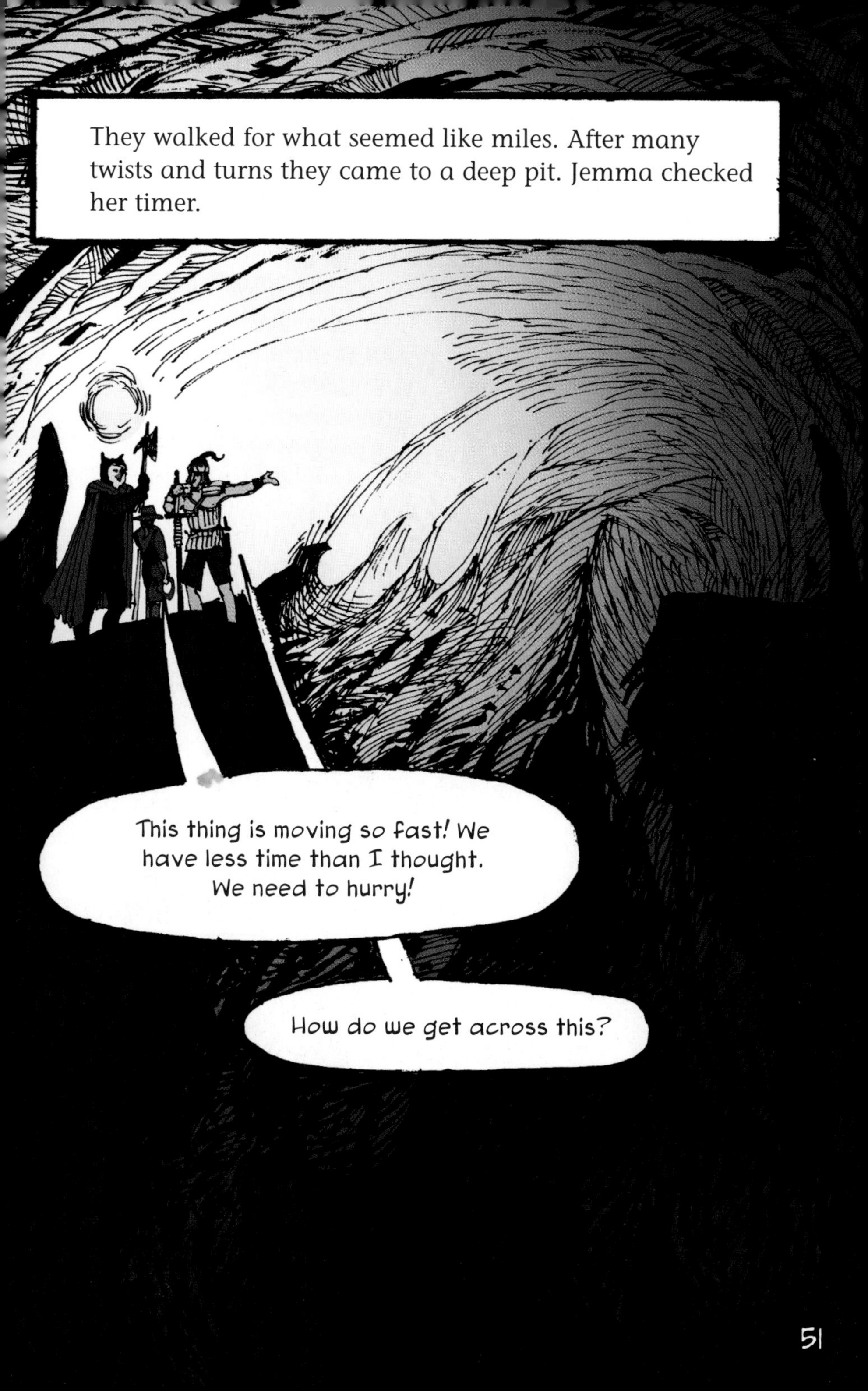
They walked for what seemed like miles. After many twists and turns they came to a deep pit. Jemma checked her timer.
This thing is moving so fast! We have less time than I thought. We need to hurry!
How do we get across this?

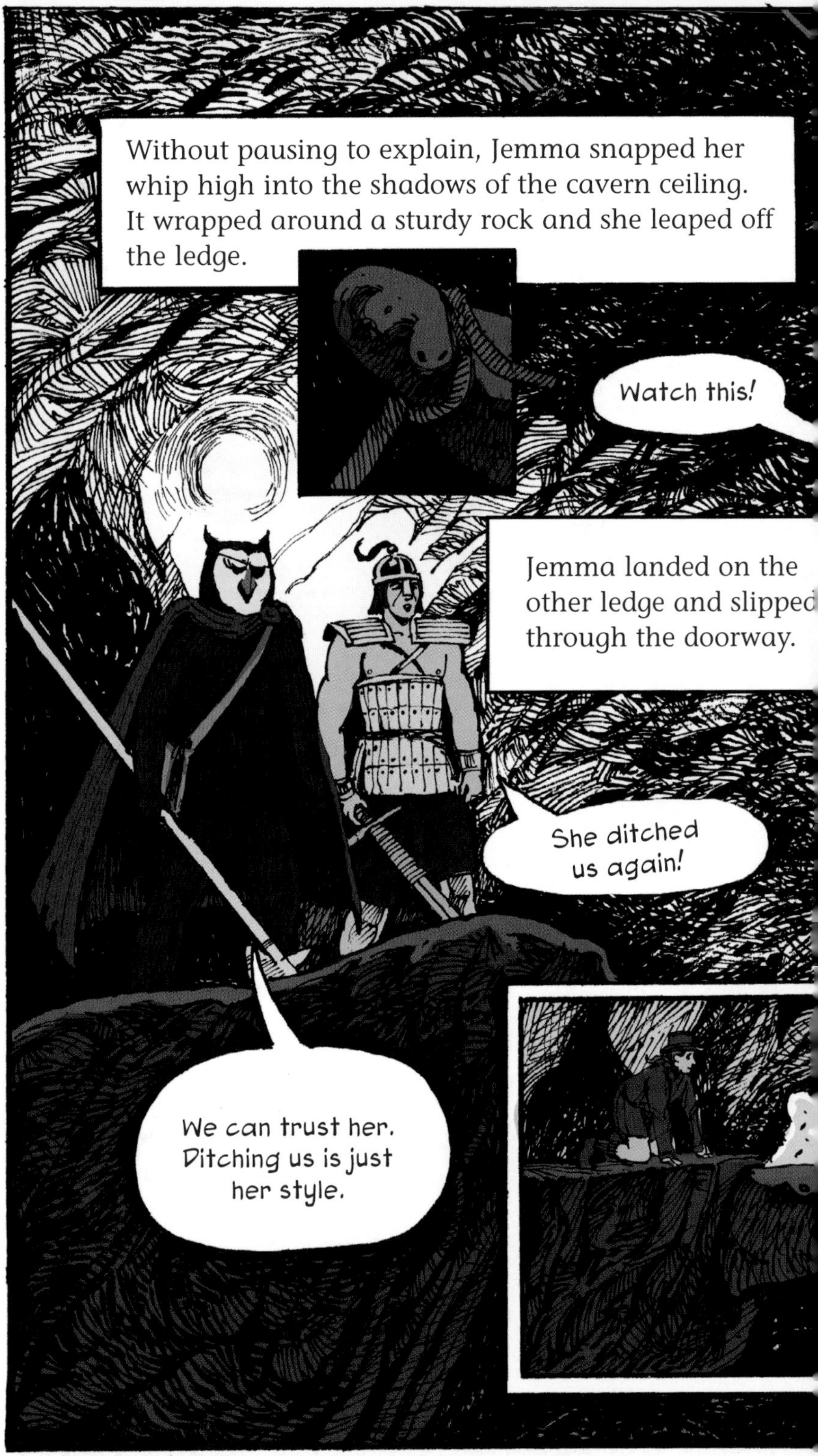
Without pausing to explain, Jemma snapped her whip high into the shadows of the cavern ceiling. It wrapped around a sturdy rock and she leaped off the ledge.
Watch this!
Jemma landed on the other ledge and slipped through the doorway.
She ditched us again!
We can trust her. Ditching us is just her style.

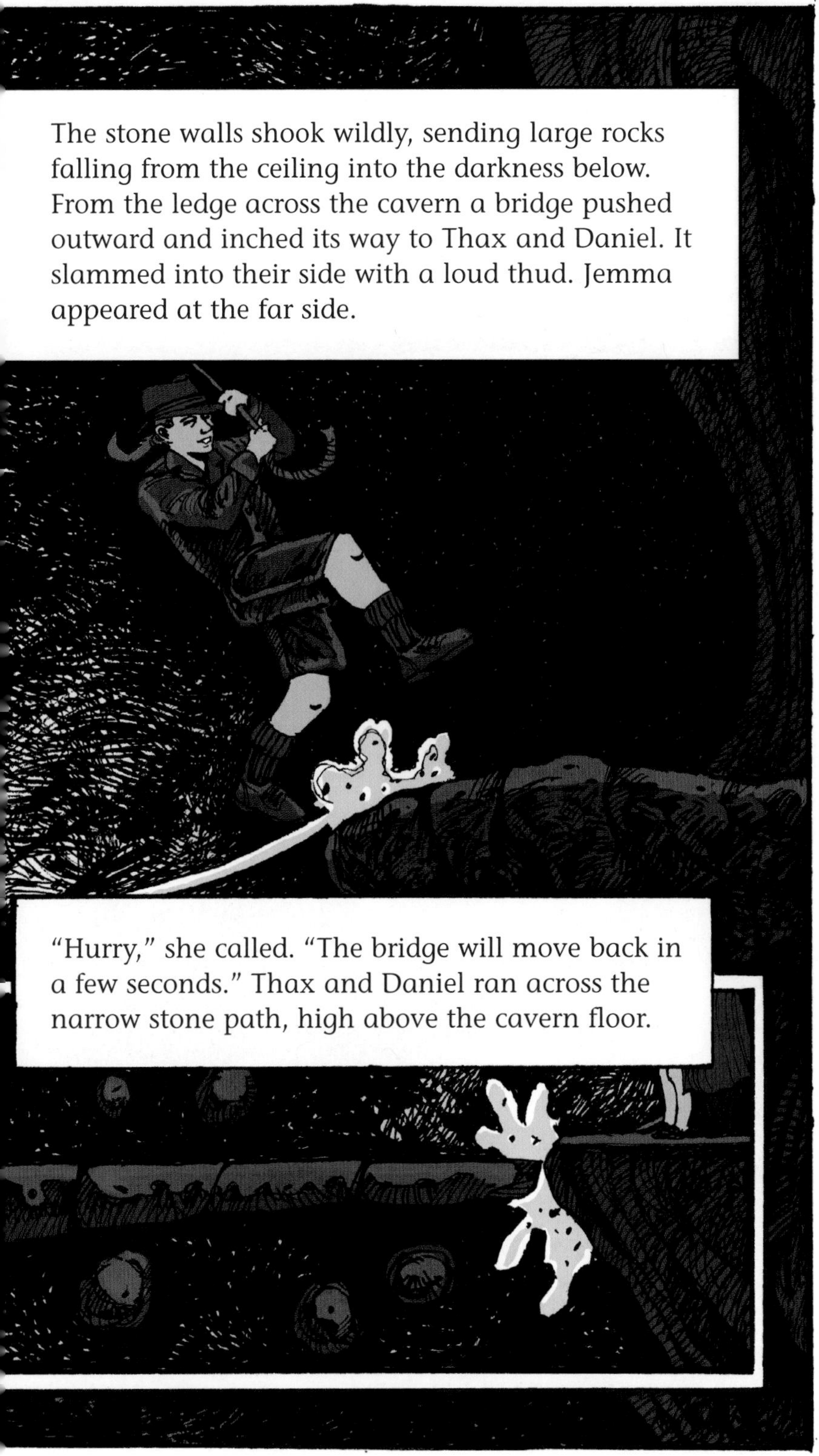
The stone walls shook wildly, sending large rocks falling from the ceiling into the darkness below. From the ledge across the cavern a bridge pushed outward and inched its way to Thax and Daniel. It slammed into their side with a loud thud. Jemma appeared at the far side.
"Hurry," she called. "The bridge will move back in a few seconds." Thax and Daniel ran across the narrow stone path, high above the cavern floor.

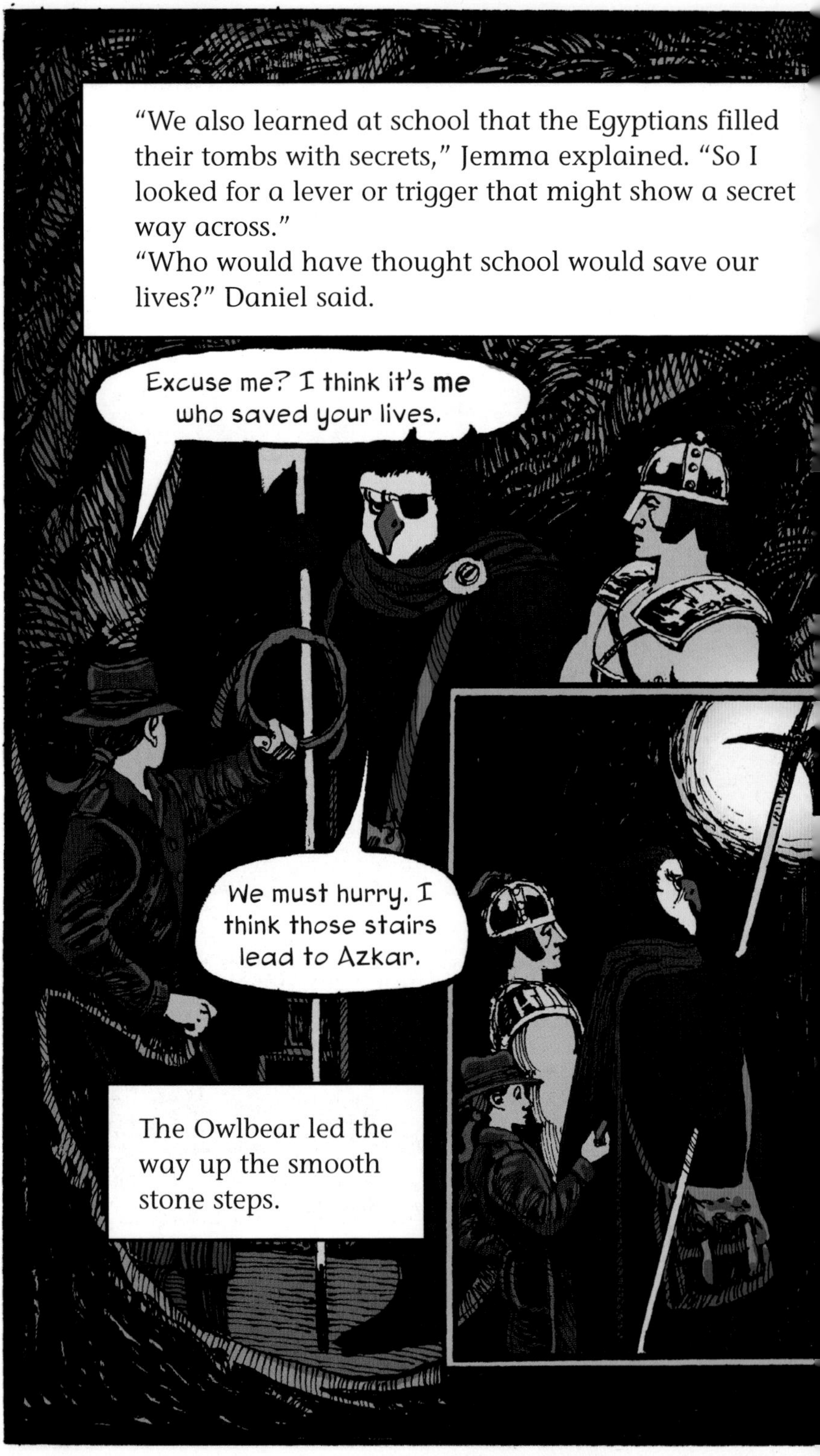
"We also learned at school that the Egyptians filled their tombs with secrets," Jemma explained. "So I looked for a lever or trigger that might show a secret way across."
"Who would have thought school would save our lives?" Daniel said.
Excuse me? I think it's **me** who saved your lives.
We must hurry. I think those stairs lead to Azkar.
The Owlbear led the way up the smooth stone steps.

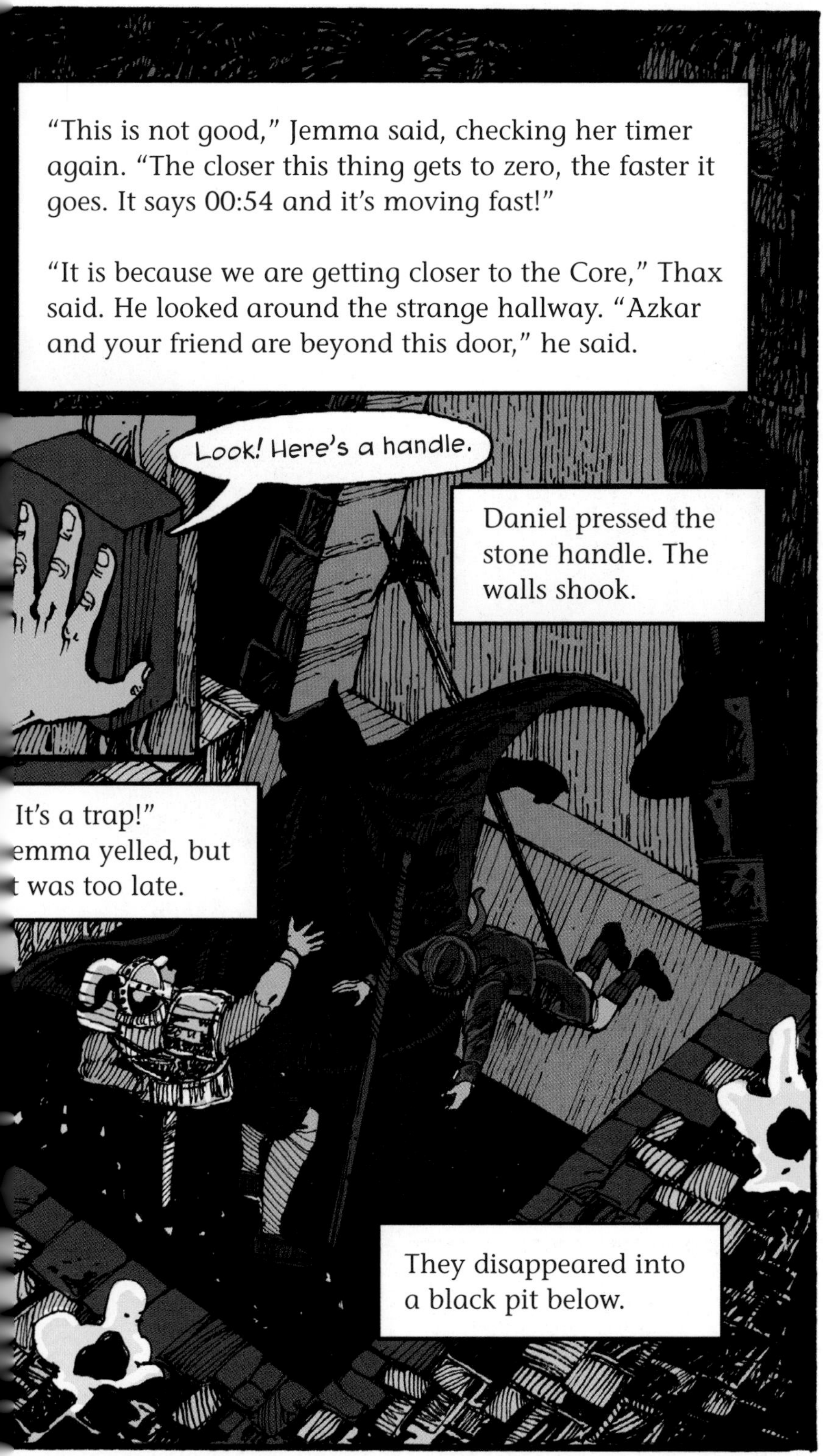
"This is not good," Jemma said, checking her timer again. "The closer this thing gets to zero, the faster it goes. It says 00:54 and it's moving fast!"
"It is because we are getting closer to the Core," Thax said. He looked around the strange hallway. "Azkar and your friend are beyond this door," he said.
Look! Here's a handle.
Daniel pressed the stone handle. The walls shook.
It's a trap!" emma yelled, but t was too late.
They disappeared into a black pit below.

Chapter NINE

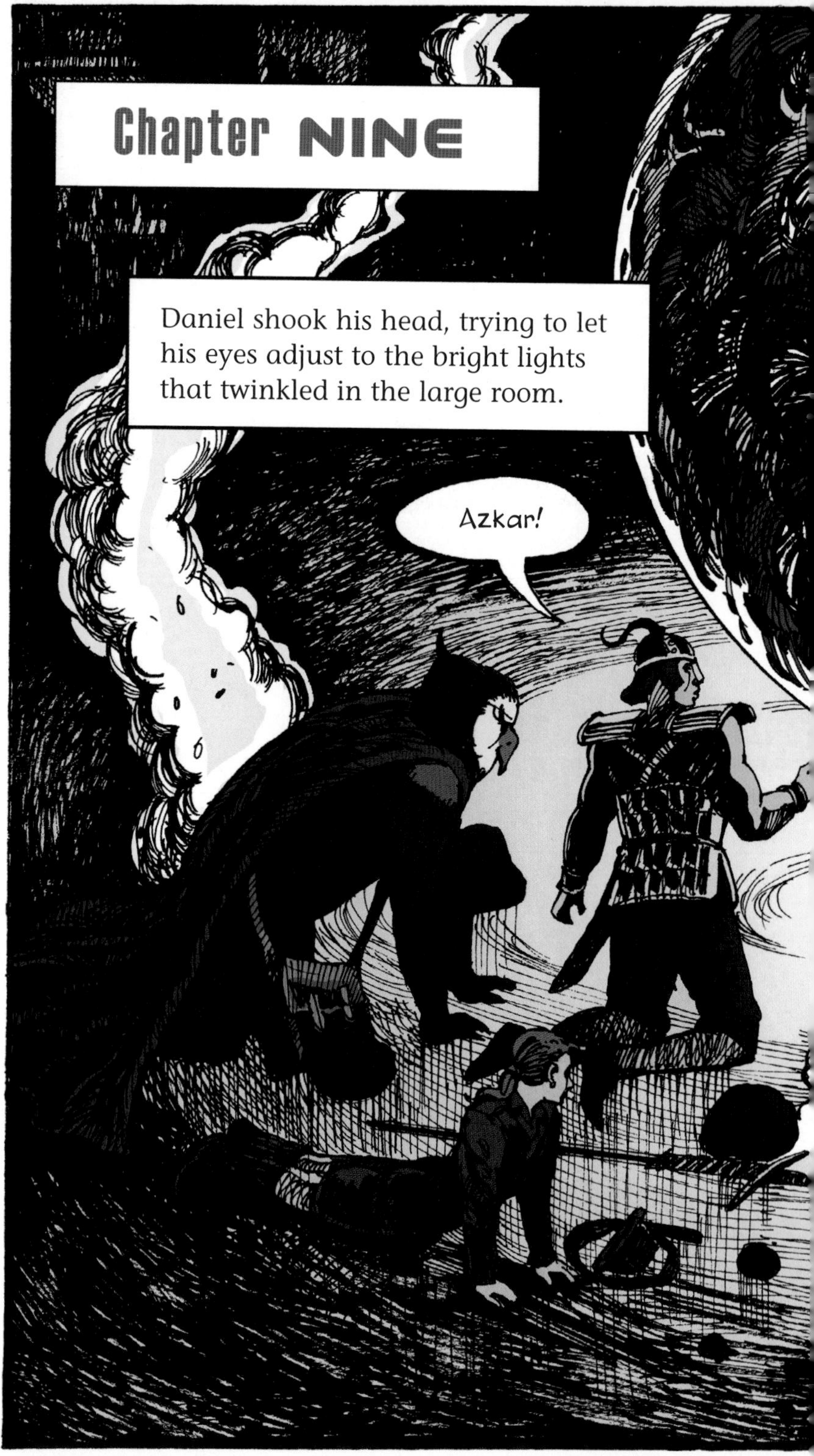
Daniel shook his head, trying to let his eyes adjust to the bright lights that twinkled in the large room.
Azkar!

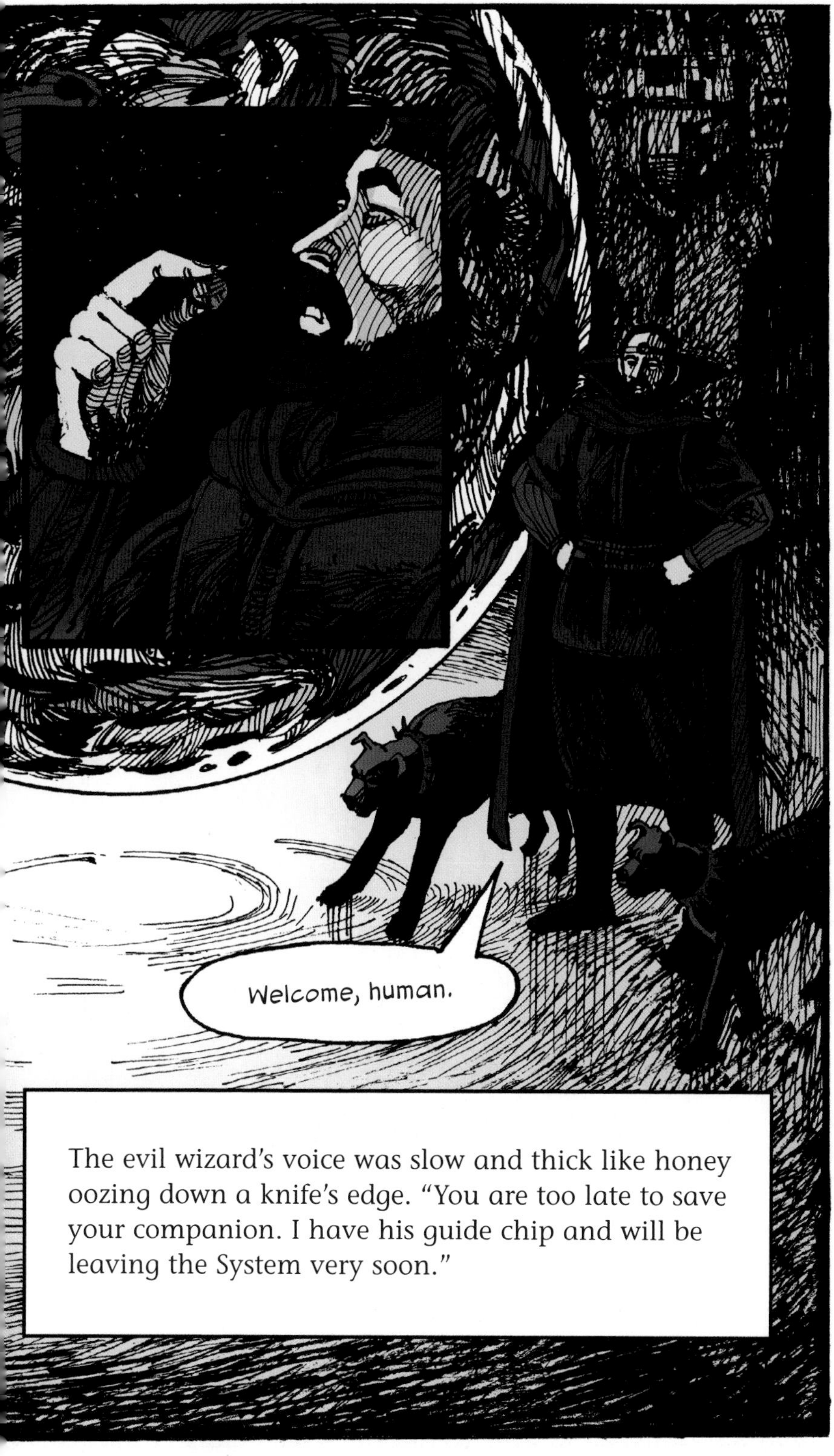
Welcome, human.
The evil wizard's voice was slow and thick like honey oozing down a knife's edge. "You are too late to save your companion. I have his guide chip and will be leaving the System very soon."

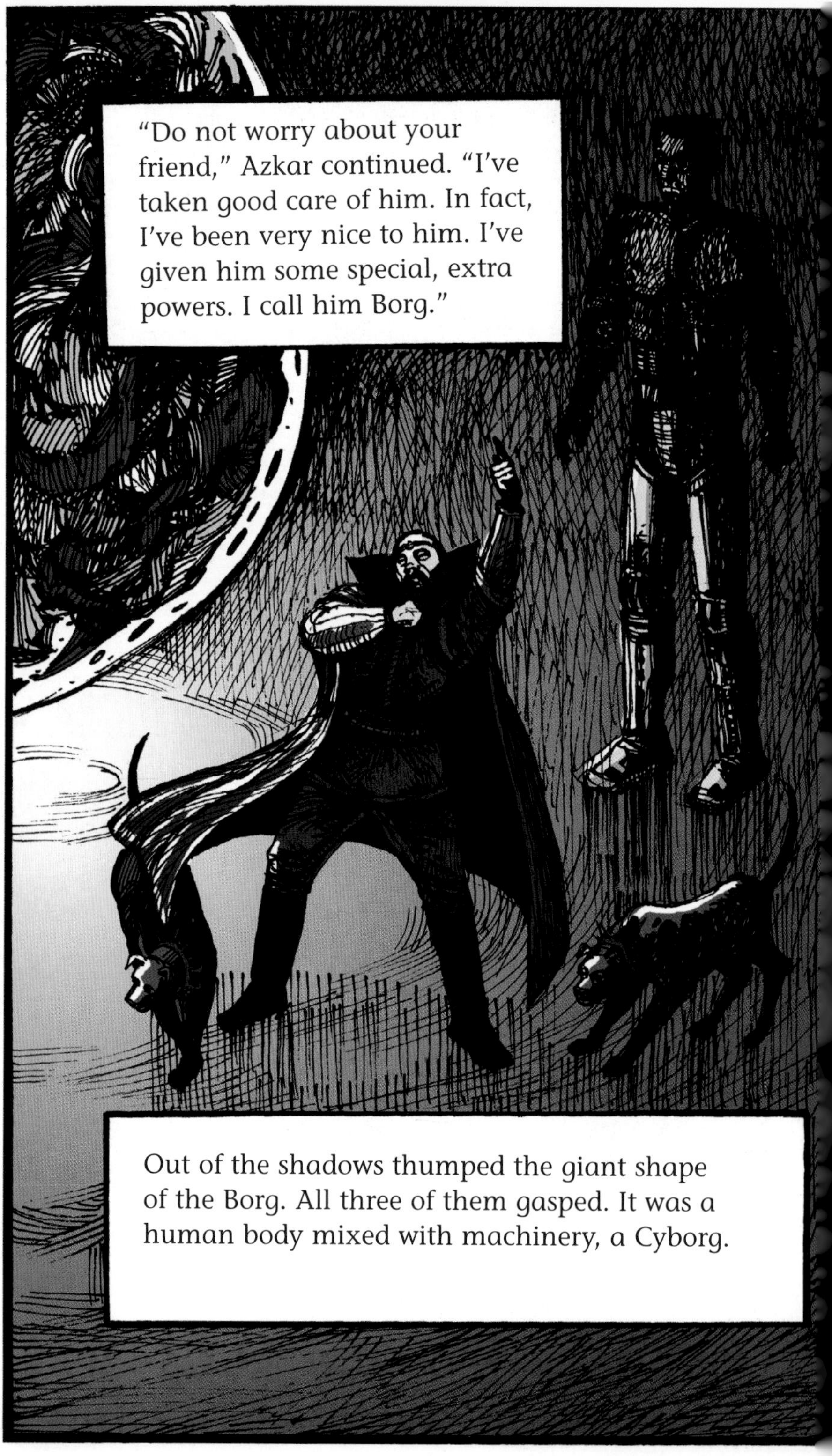
"Do not worry about your friend," Azkar continued. "I've taken good care of him. In fact, I've been very nice to him. I've given him some special, extra powers. I call him Borg."
Out of the shadows thumped the giant shape of the Borg. All three of them gasped. It was a human body mixed with machinery, a Cyborg.

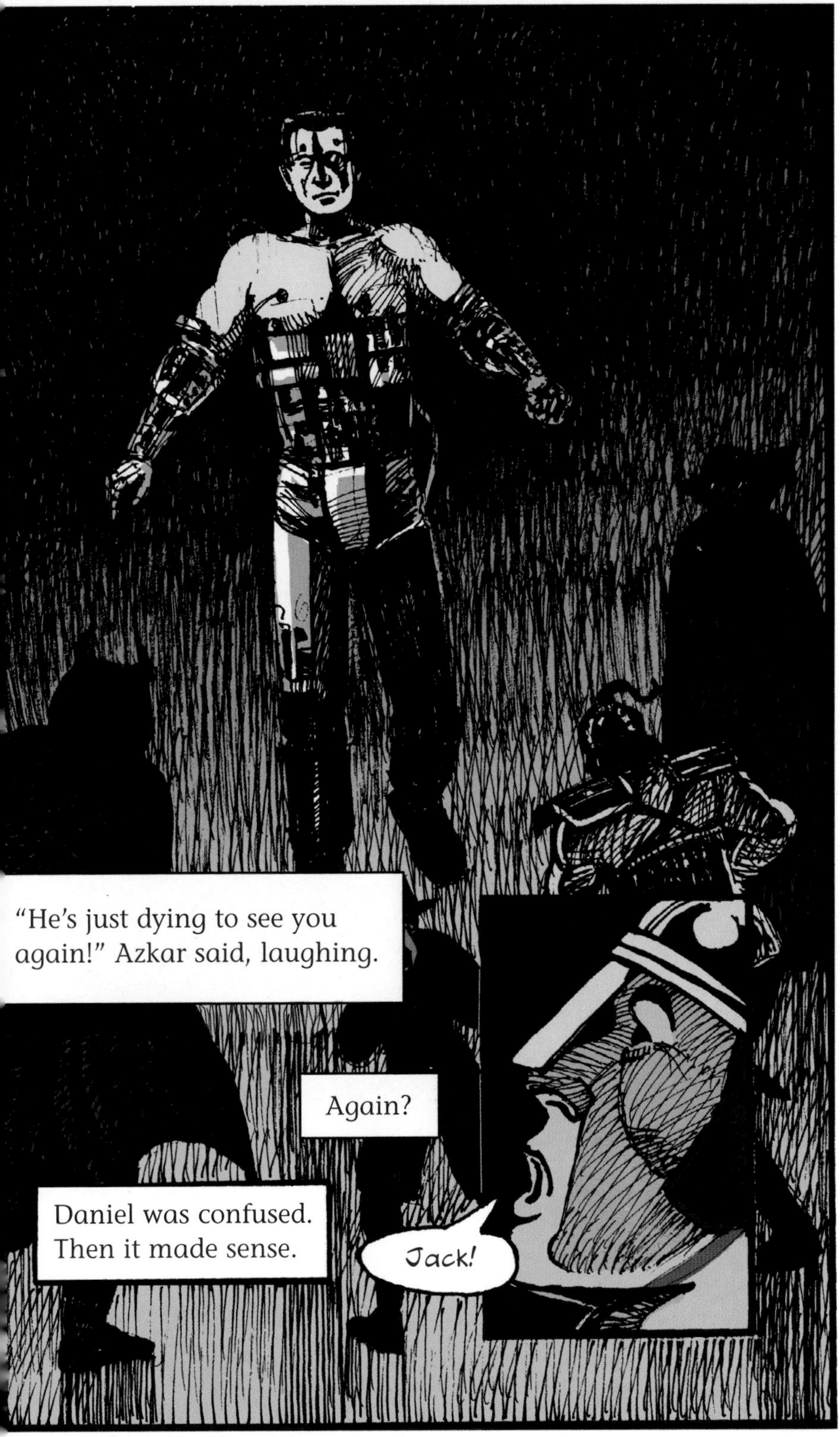
"He's just dying to see you
again!" Azkar said, laughing.
Again?
Daniel was confused.
Then it made sense.
Jack!

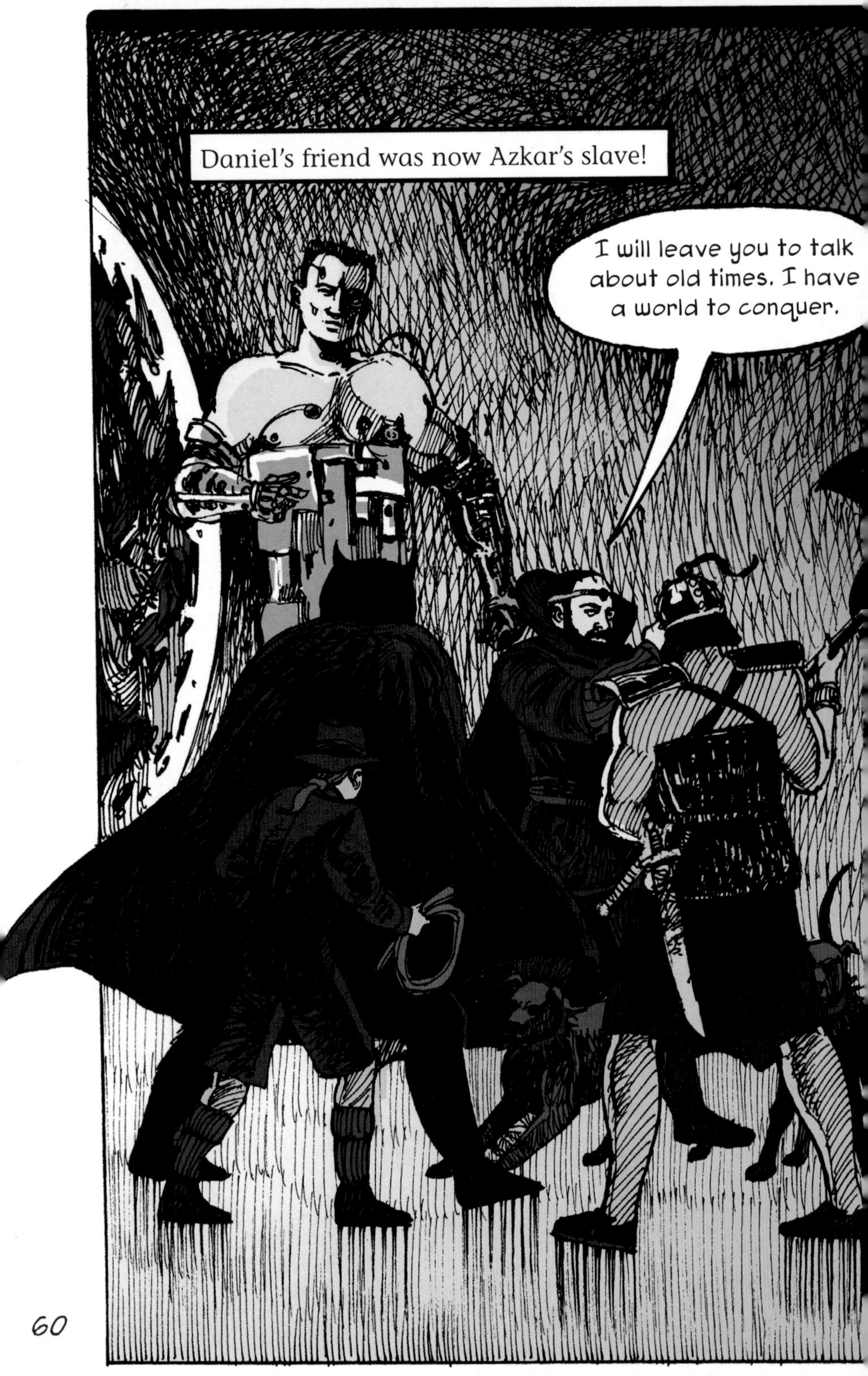
Daniel's friend was now Azkar's slave!
I will leave you to talk about old times. I have a world to conquer.

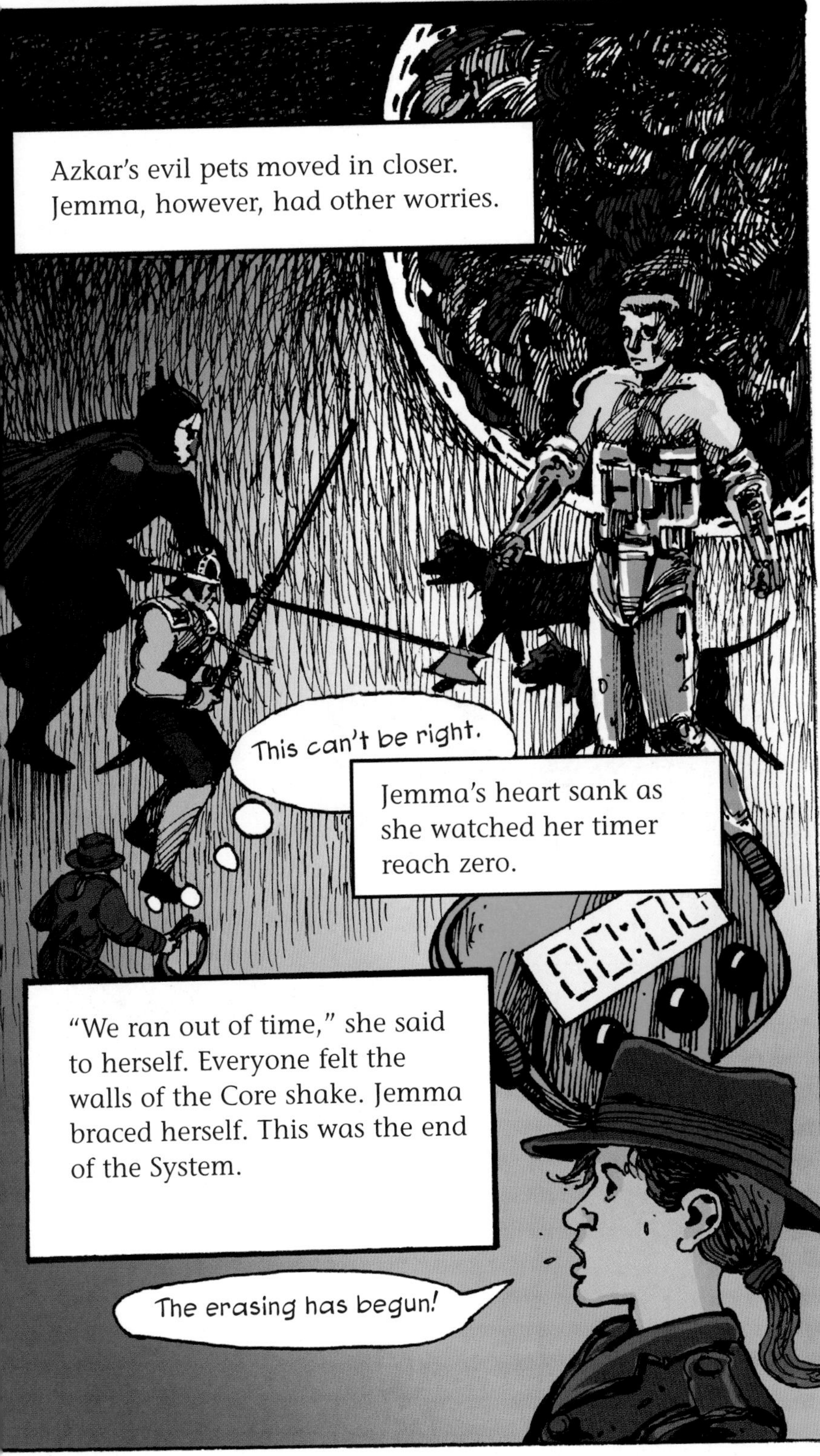
Azkar's evil pets moved in closer. Jemma, however, had other worries.
This can't be right.
Jemma's heart sank as she watched her timer reach zero.
"We ran out of time," she said to herself. Everyone felt the walls of the Core shake. Jemma braced herself. This was the end of the System.
The erasing has begun!

Chapter TEN

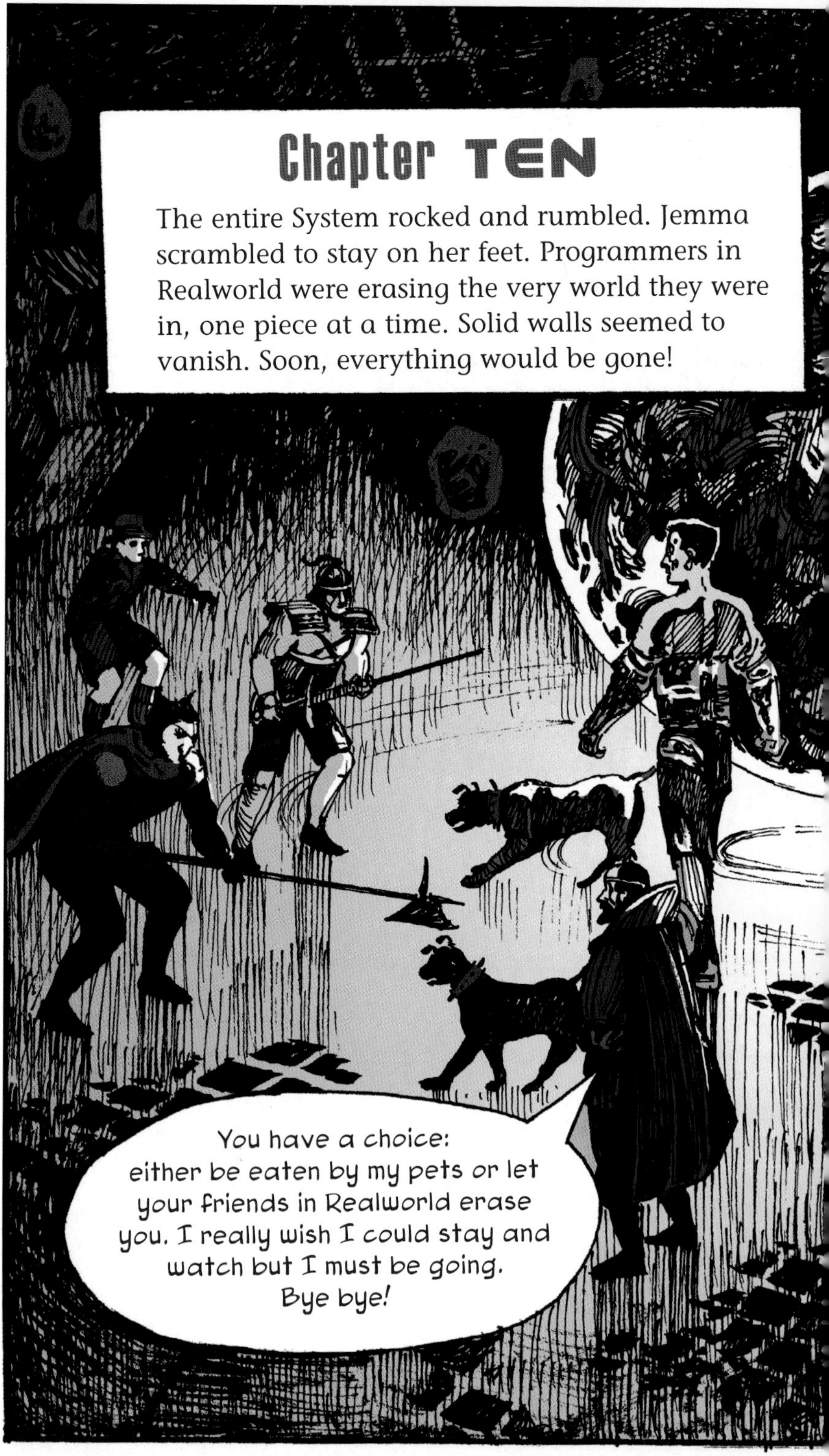

The entire System rocked and rumbled. Jemma scrambled to stay on her feet. Programmers in Realworld were erasing the very world they were in, one piece at a time. Solid walls seemed to vanish. Soon, everything would be gone!
You have a choice: either be eaten by my pets or let your friends in Realworld erase you. I really wish I could stay and watch but I must be going. Bye bye!

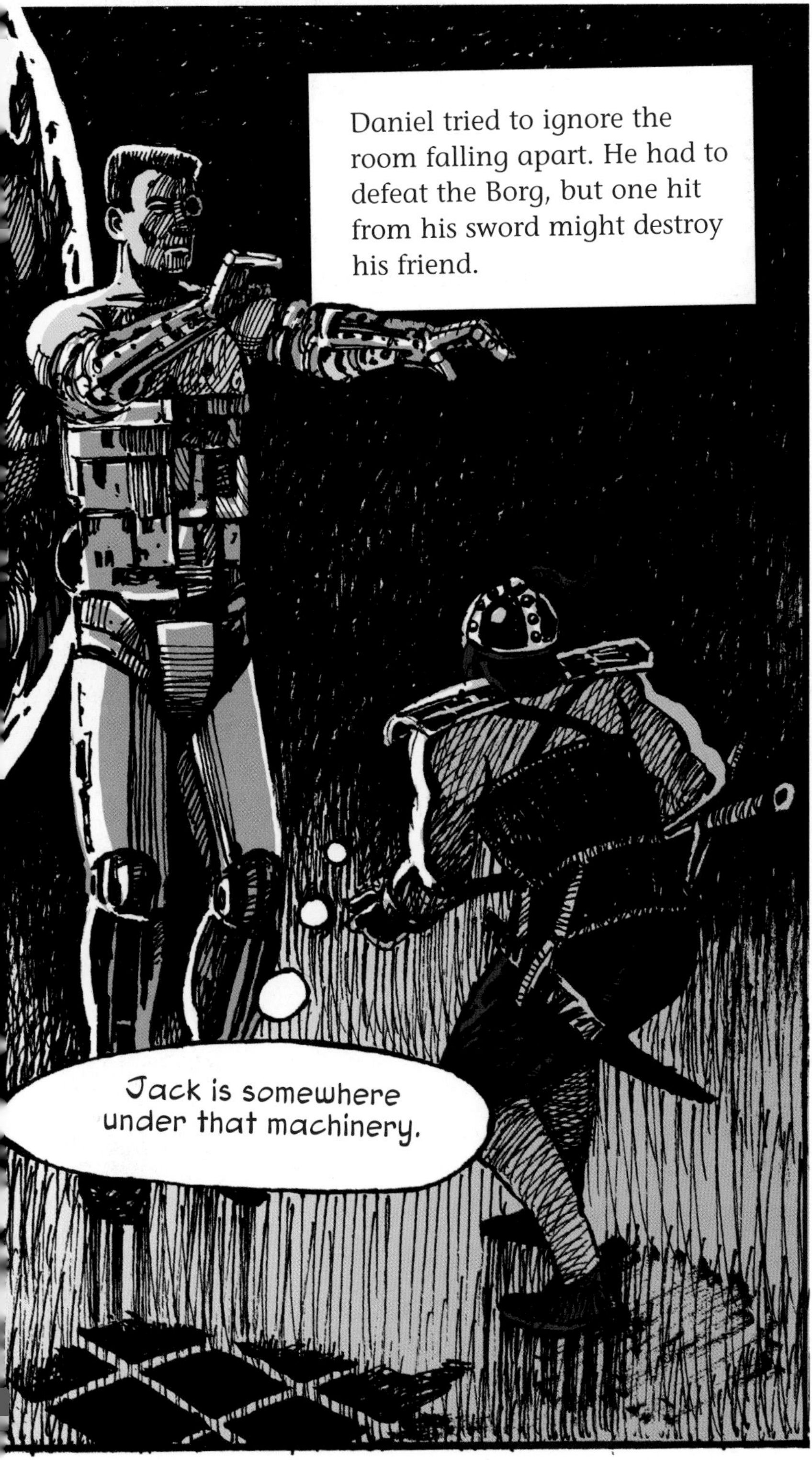
Daniel tried to ignore the room falling apart. He had to defeat the Borg, but one hit from his sword might destroy his friend.
Jack is somewhere under that machinery.

Thax and Jemma huddled together as the data hounds slowly moved in closer.

"Azkar plans to use this destruction to confuse people in the real world. Then he will slip into your world without being seen!" said Thax.

"We have to stop him from using Jack's guide chip," Jemma said.

Quickly, she cracked her whip toward the rocks above and launched herself at the data hounds.

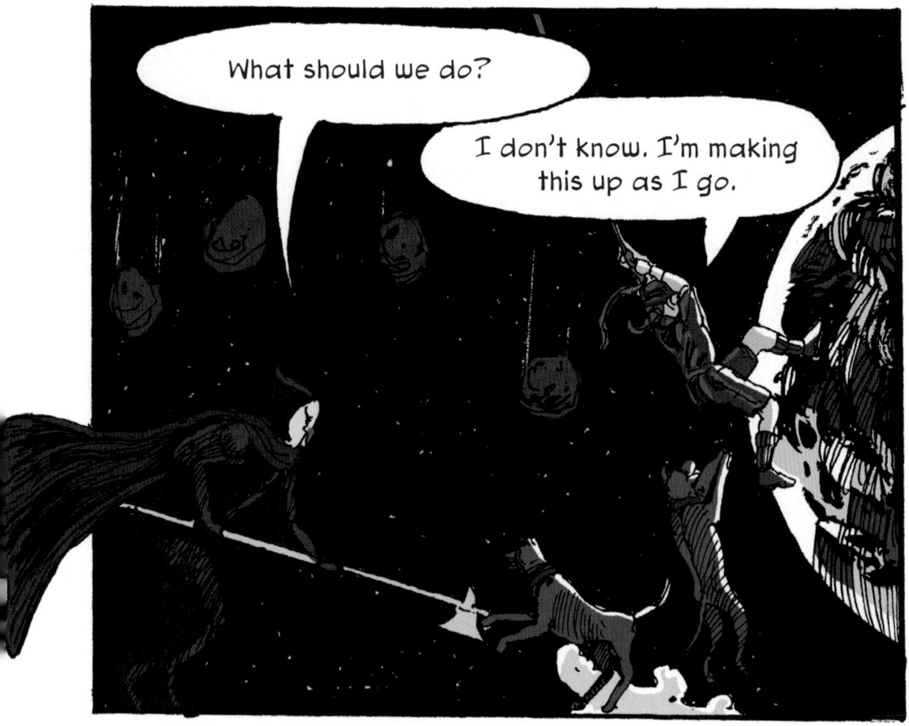
What should we do?
I don't know. I'm making this up as I go.

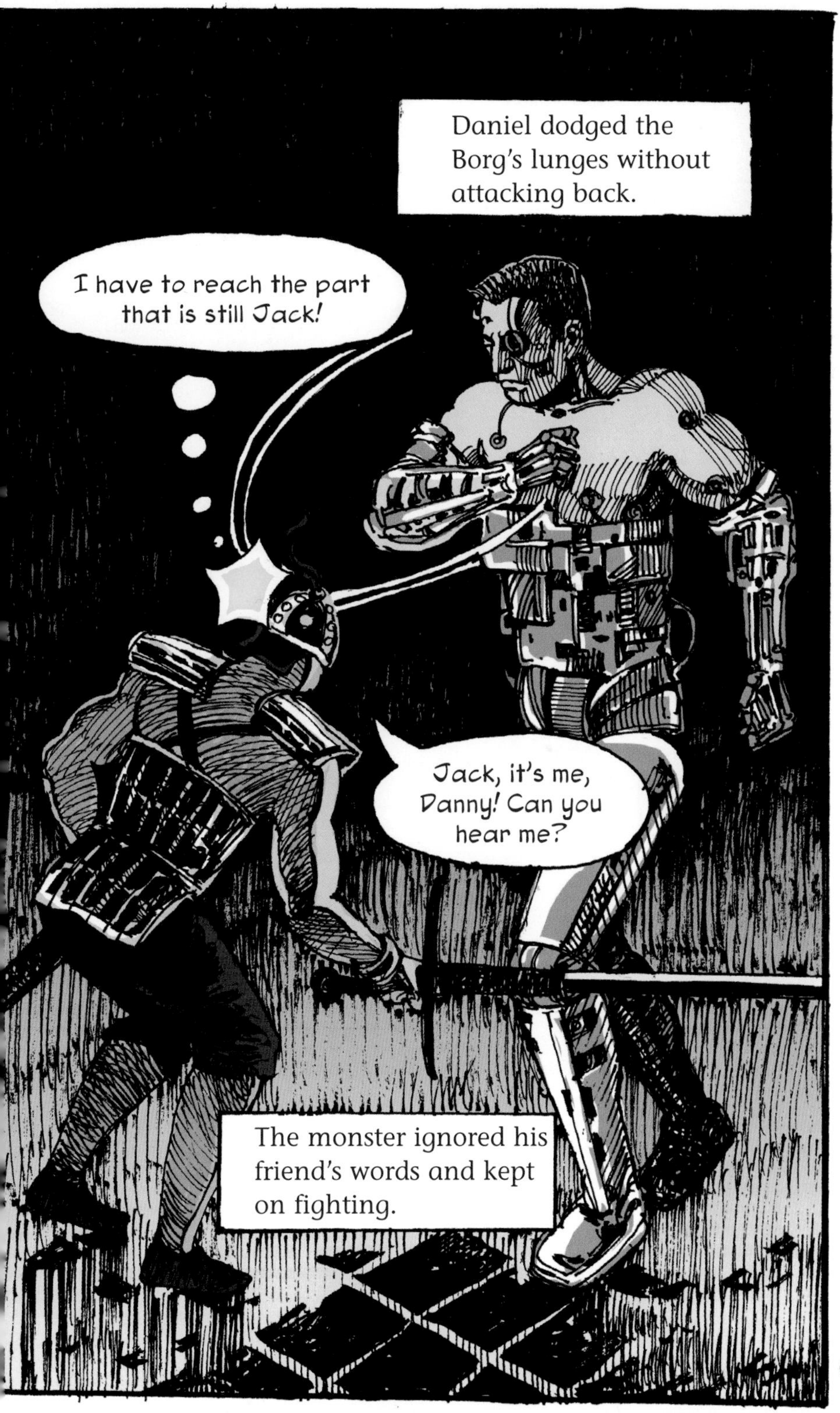
Daniel dodged the Borg's lunges without attacking back.
I have to reach the part that is still Jack!
Jack, it's me, Danny! Can you hear me?
The monster ignored his friend's words and kept on fighting.

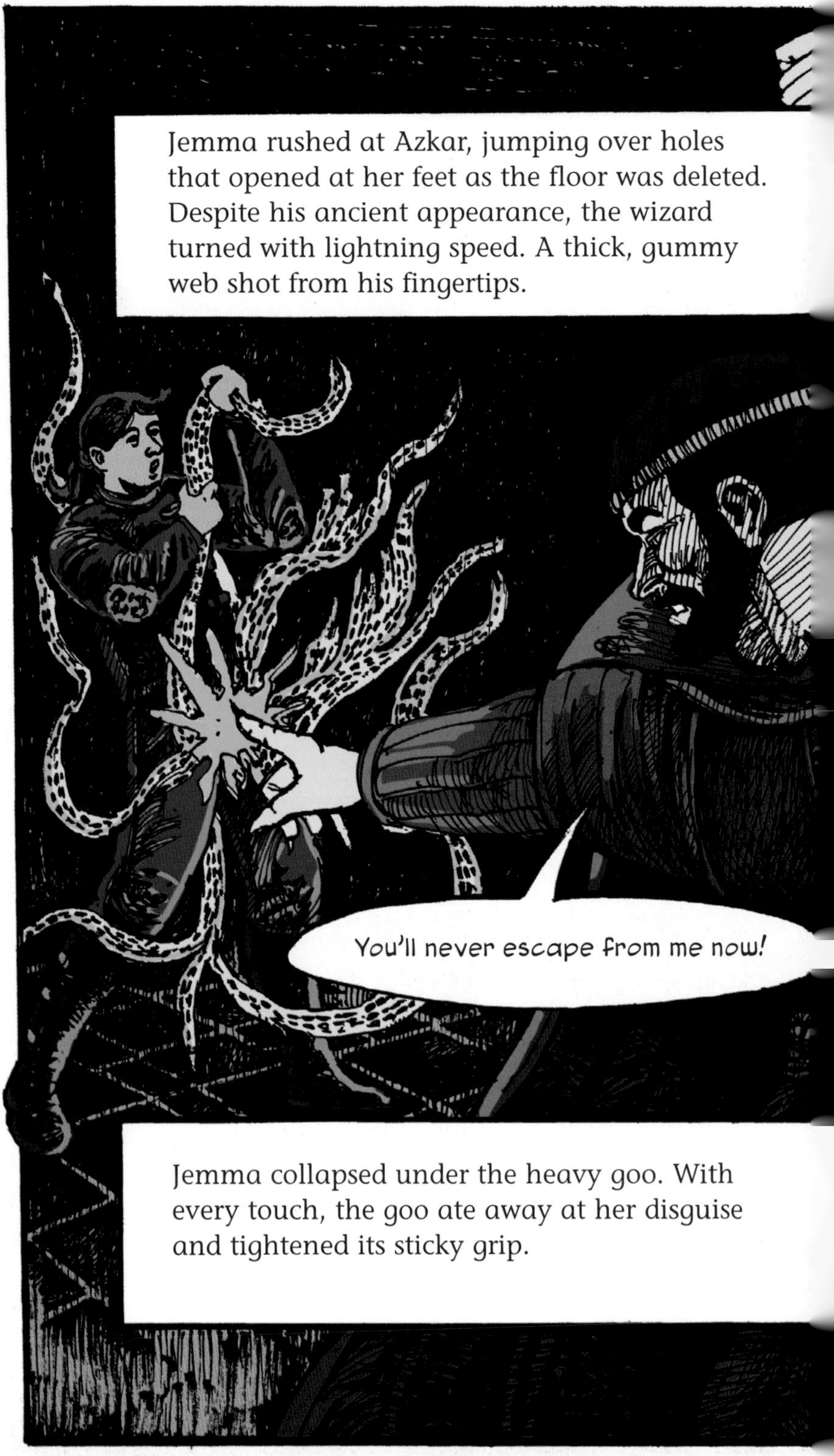
Jemma rushed at Azkar, jumping over holes that opened at her feet as the floor was deleted. Despite his ancient appearance, the wizard turned with lightning speed. A thick, gummy web shot from his fingertips.
You'll never escape from me now!
Jemma collapsed under the heavy goo. With every touch, the goo ate away at her disguise and tightened its sticky grip.

Thax was trapped under the two fierce hounds. His feathery arms and legs started to vanish as the creatures attacked.

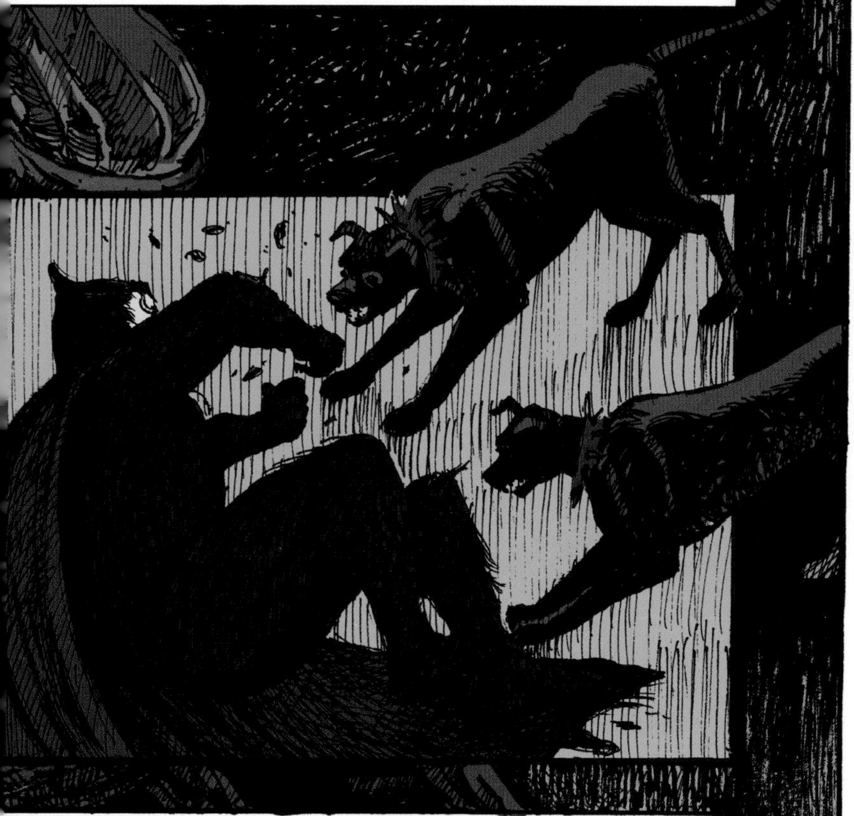

Faster and faster, holes appeared in the walls around him. With blinding speed, the evil hounds pounced on the Owlbear and quickly erased him.

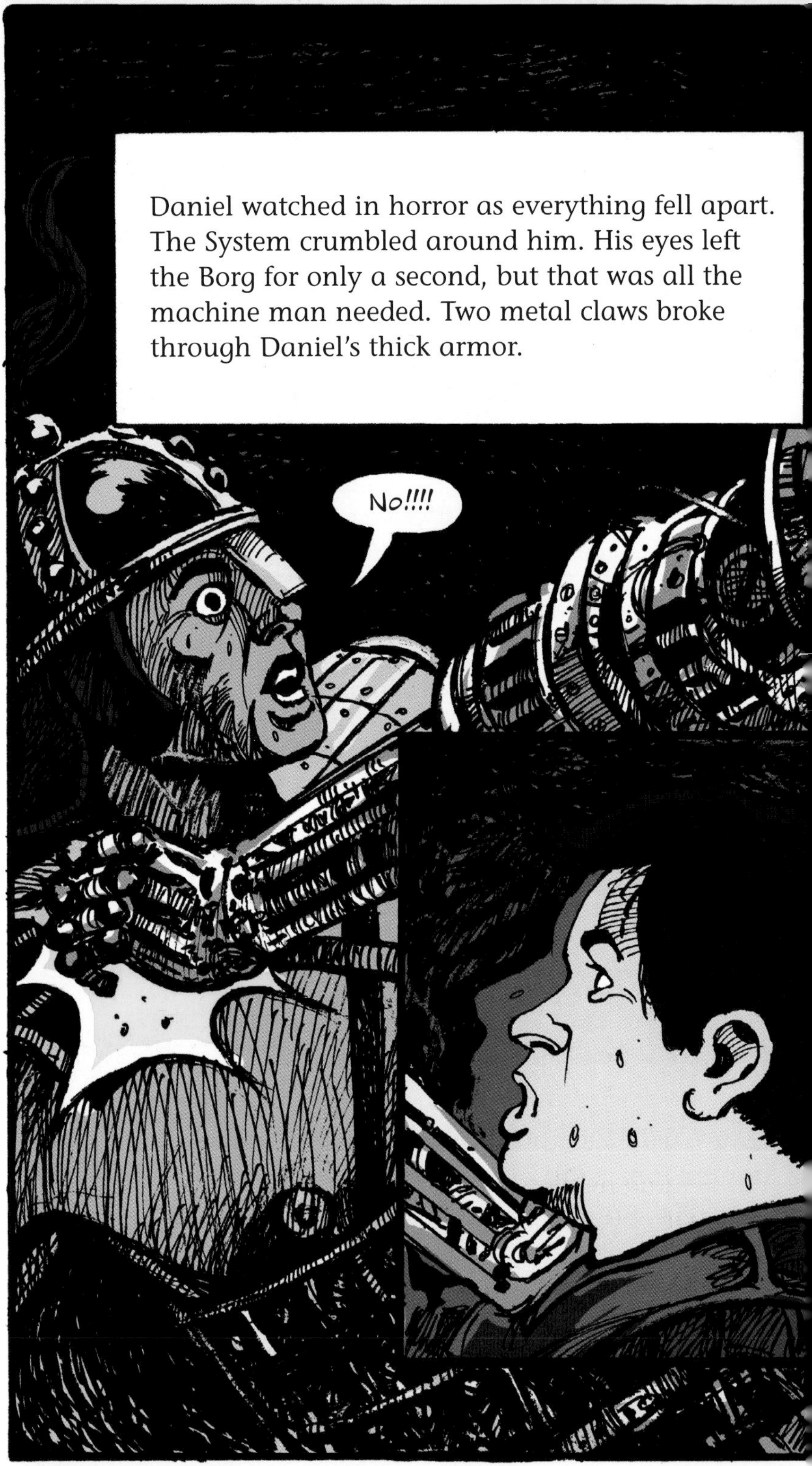
Daniel watched in horror as everything fell apart. The System crumbled around him. His eyes left the Borg for only a second, but that was all the machine man needed. Two metal claws broke through Daniel's thick armor.
No!!!!

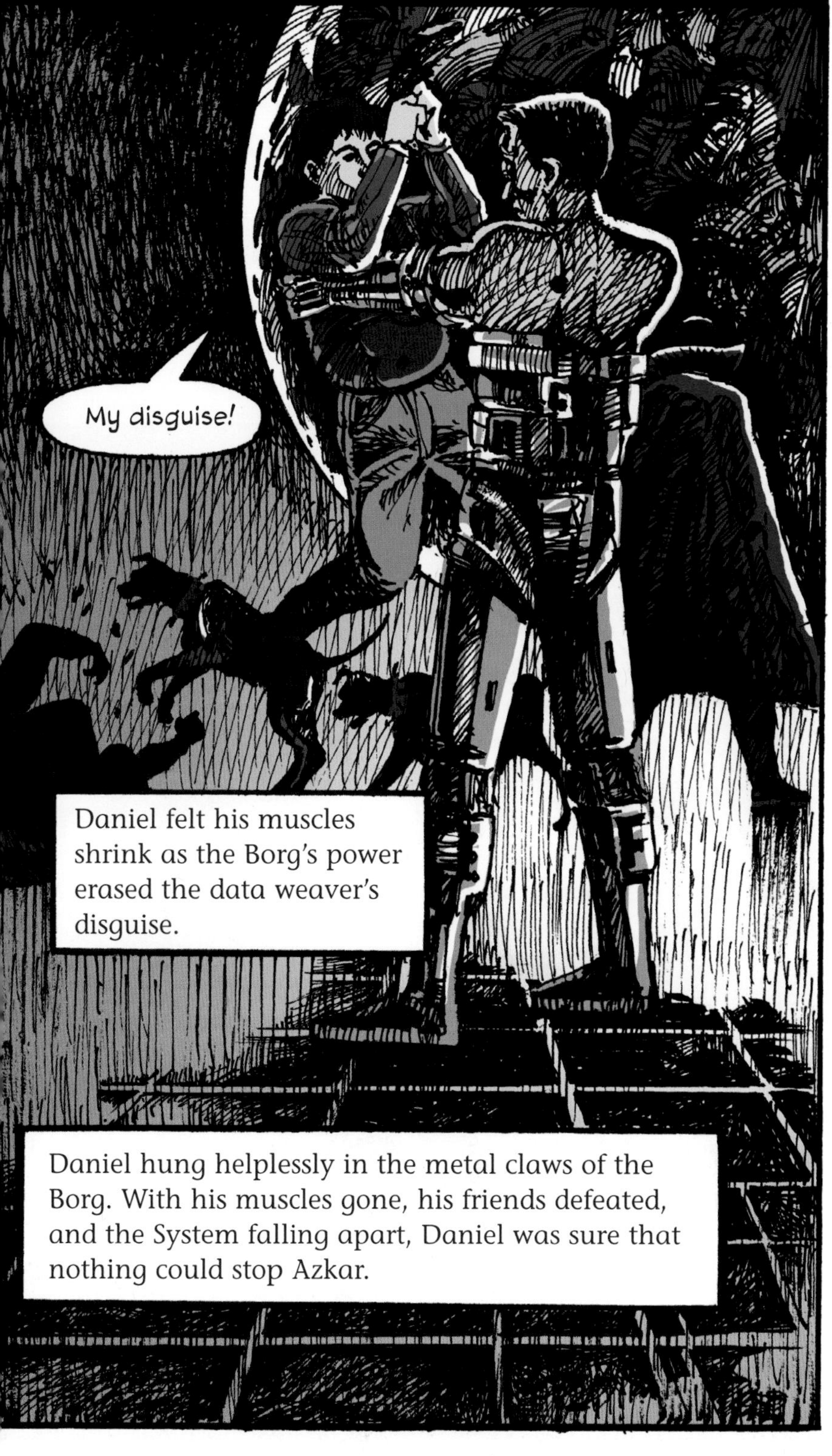
My disguise!
Daniel felt his muscles shrink as the Borg's power erased the data weaver's disguise.
Daniel hung helplessly in the metal claws of the Borg. With his muscles gone, his friends defeated, and the System falling apart, Daniel was sure that nothing could stop Azkar.

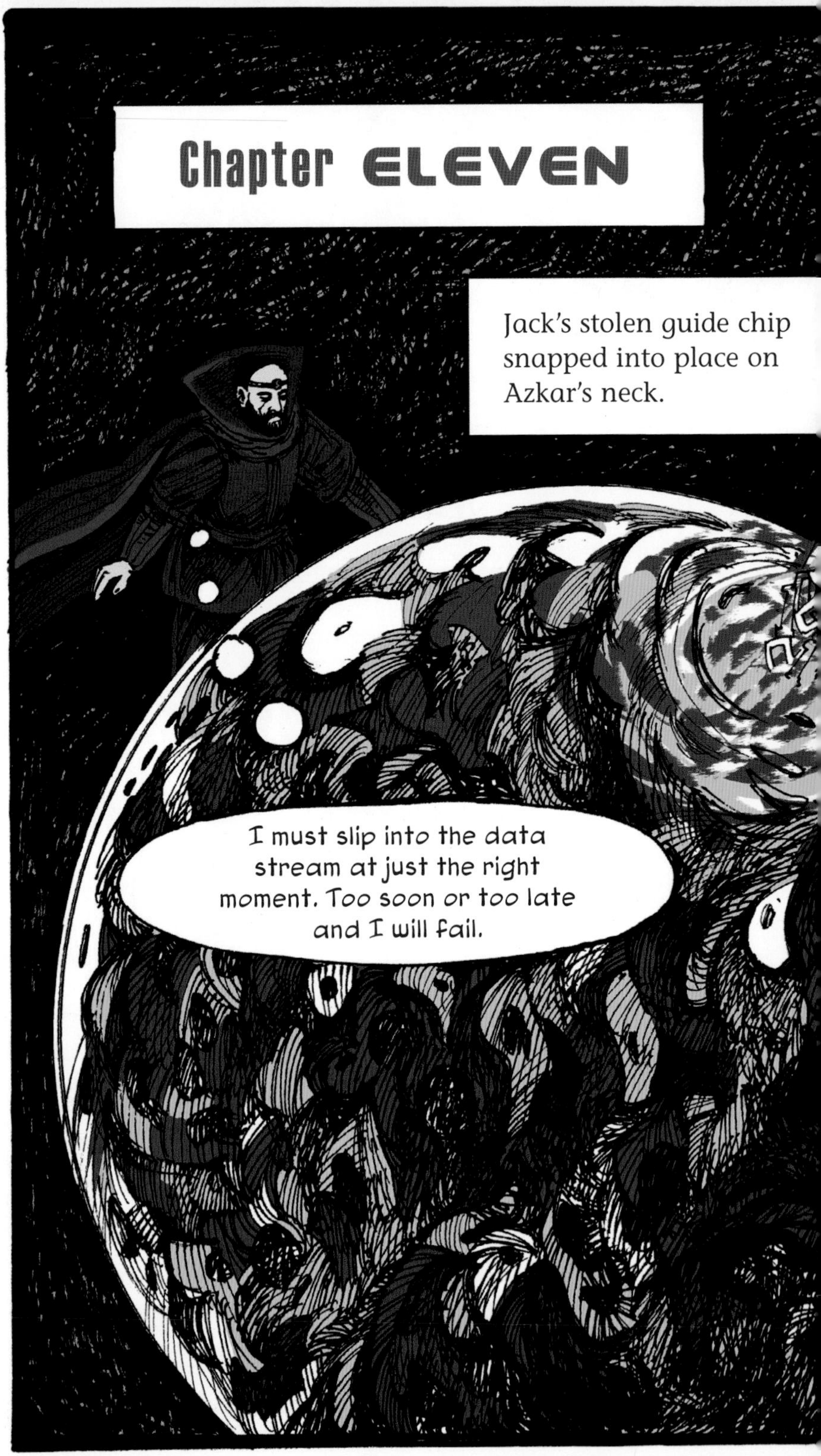
Chapter ELEVEN
Jack's stolen guide chip snapped into place on Azkar's neck.
I must slip into the data stream at just the right moment. Too soon or too late and I will fail.

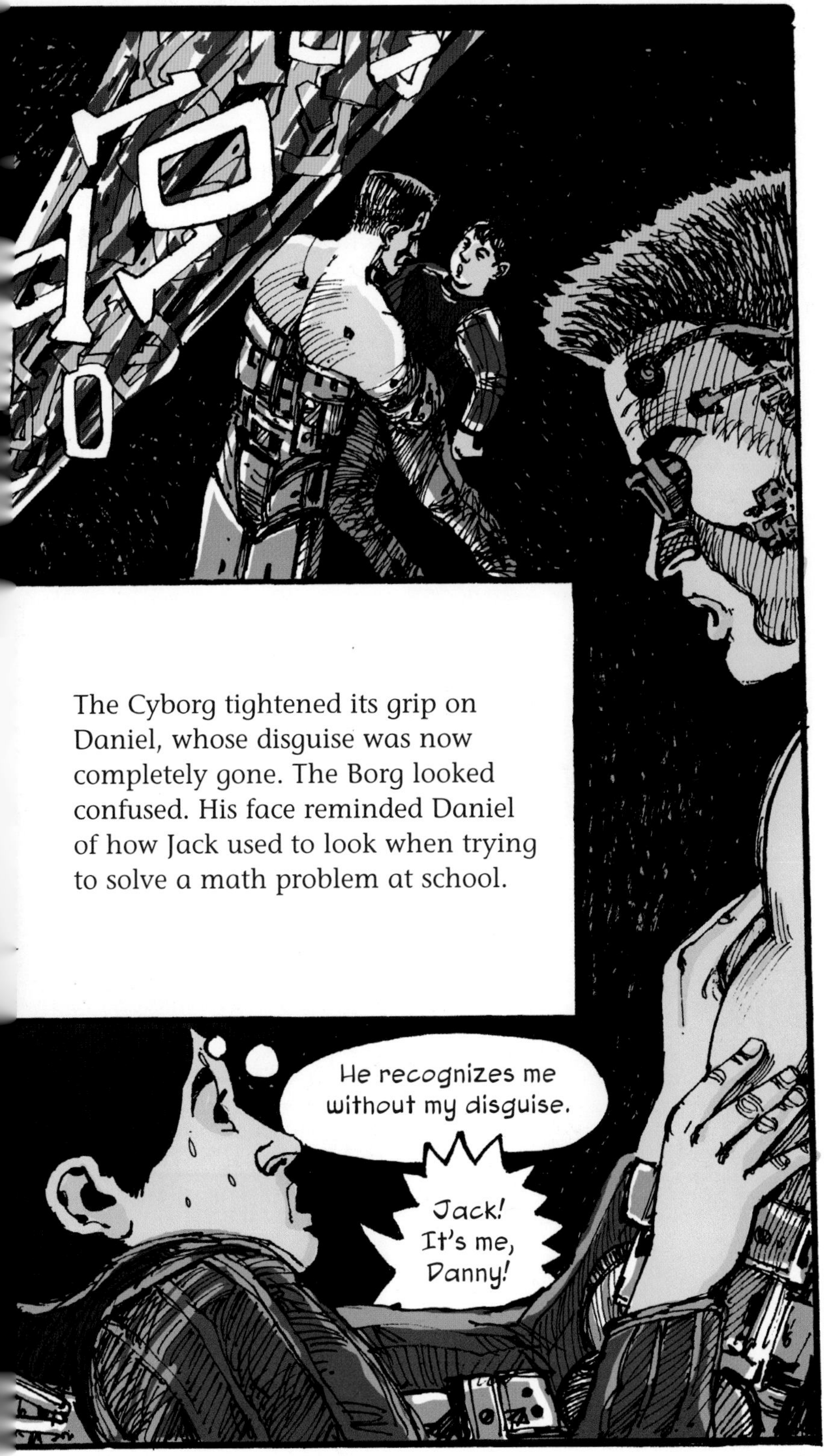
The Cyborg tightened its grip on Daniel, whose disguise was now completely gone. The Borg looked confused. His face reminded Daniel of how Jack used to look when trying to solve a math problem at school.
He recognizes me without my disguise.
Jack! It's me, Danny!

The Cyborg's expression changed once more as he whispered a name. "Danny Boy," he said.

"Don't call me Danny Boy!" Daniel yelled.

Then he changed his mind. "Call me whatever you want! It's just good to have you back, Jack."

Jack was now in complete control of his machine body. He set Daniel down on the ground.

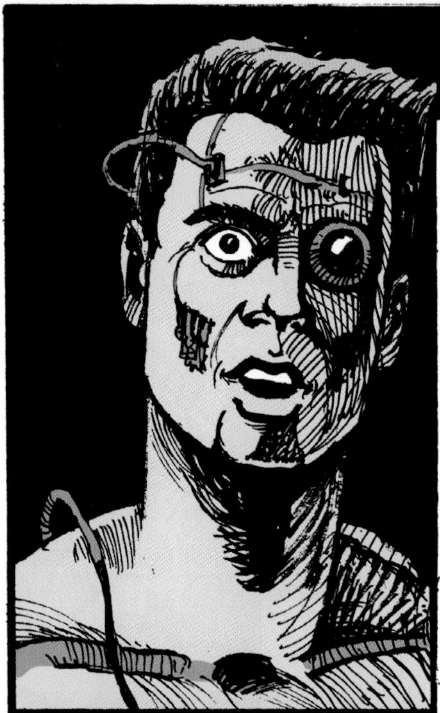

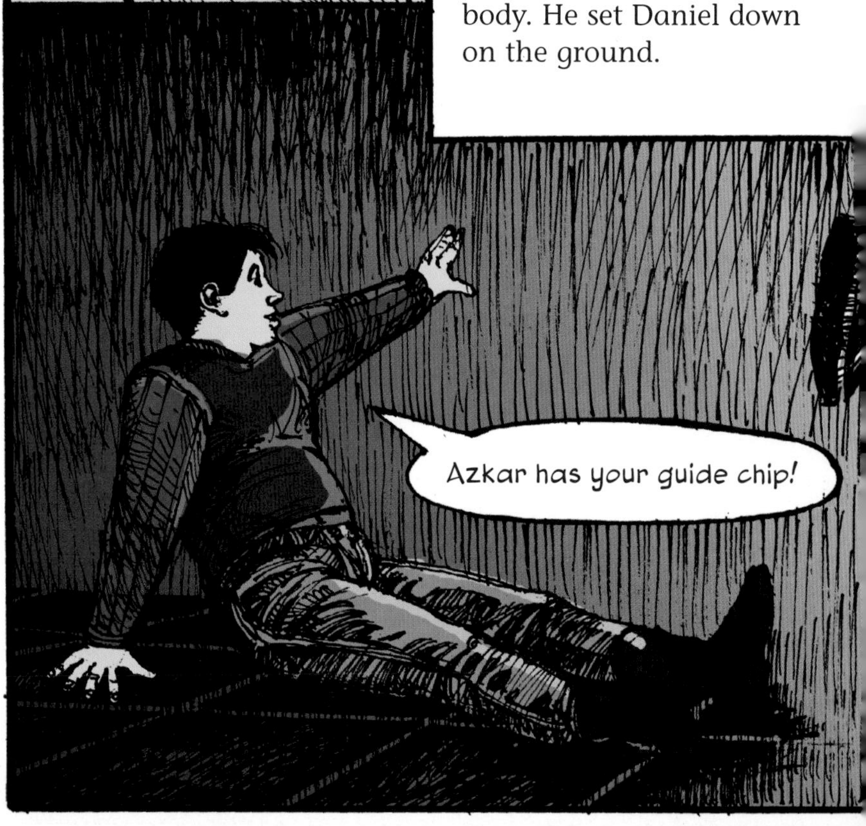
Azkar has your guide chip!

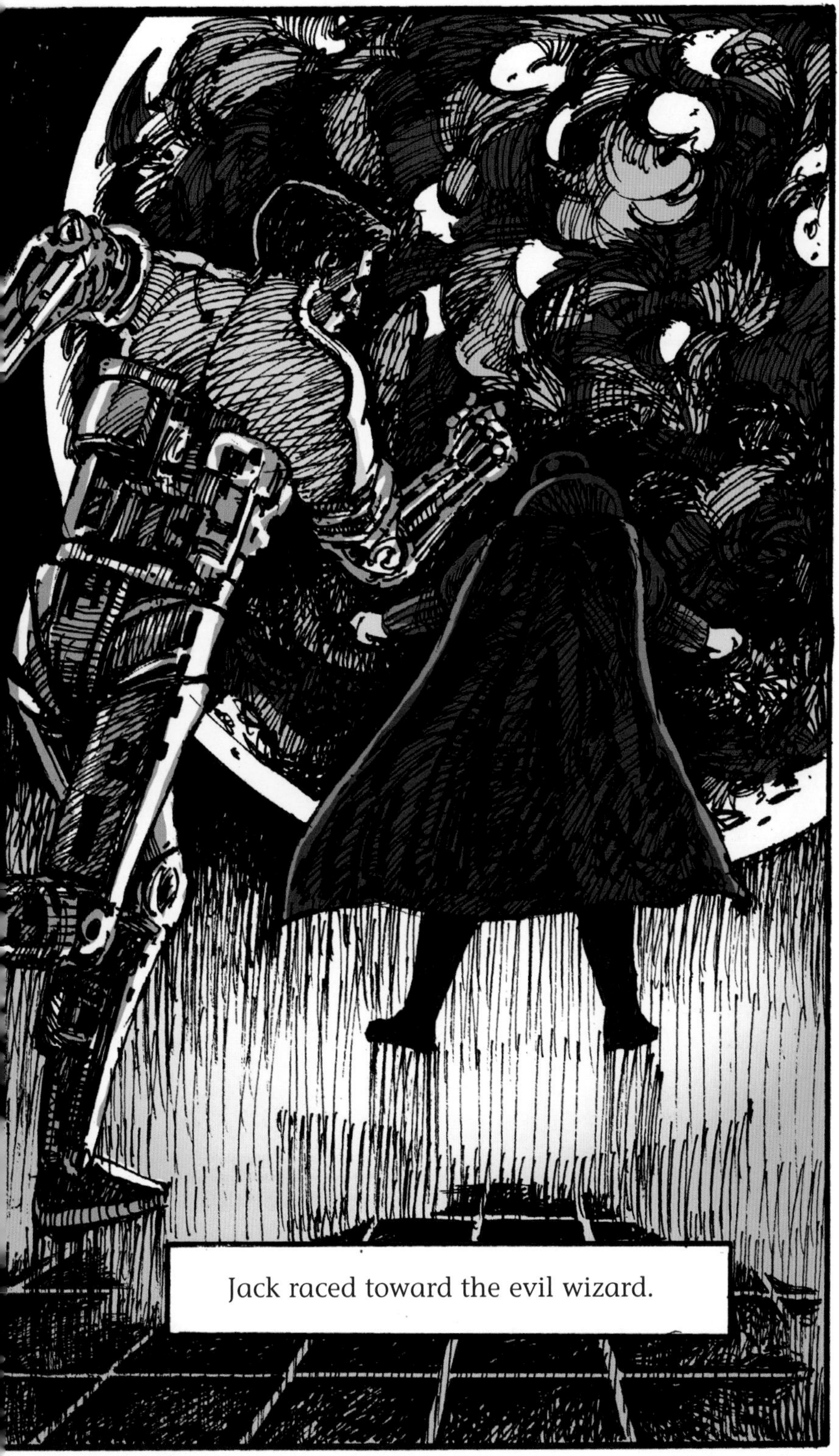
Jack raced toward the evil wizard.

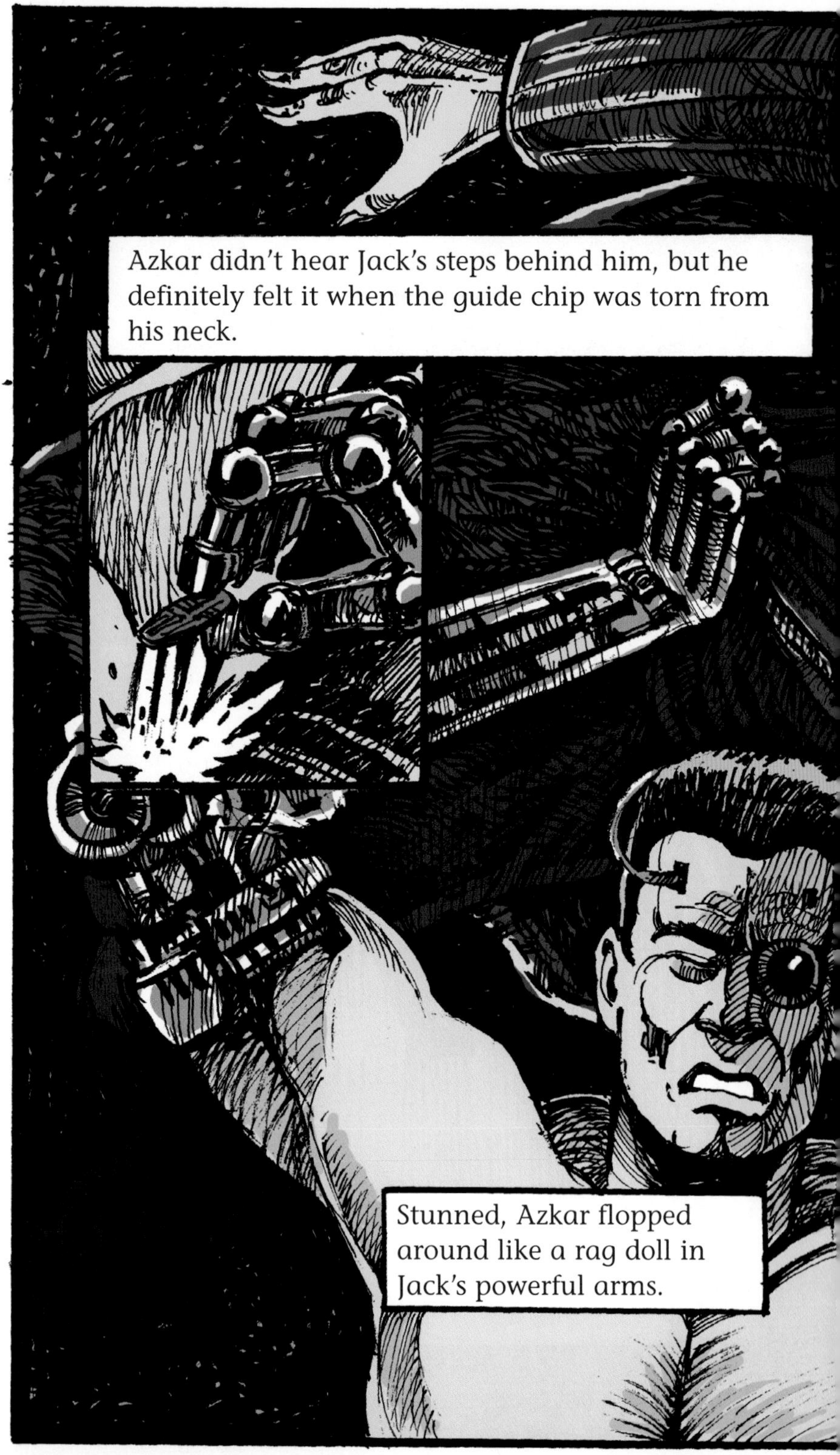
Azkar didn't hear Jack's steps behind him, but he definitely felt it when the guide chip was torn from his neck.
Stunned, Azkar flopped around like a rag doll in Jack's powerful arms.

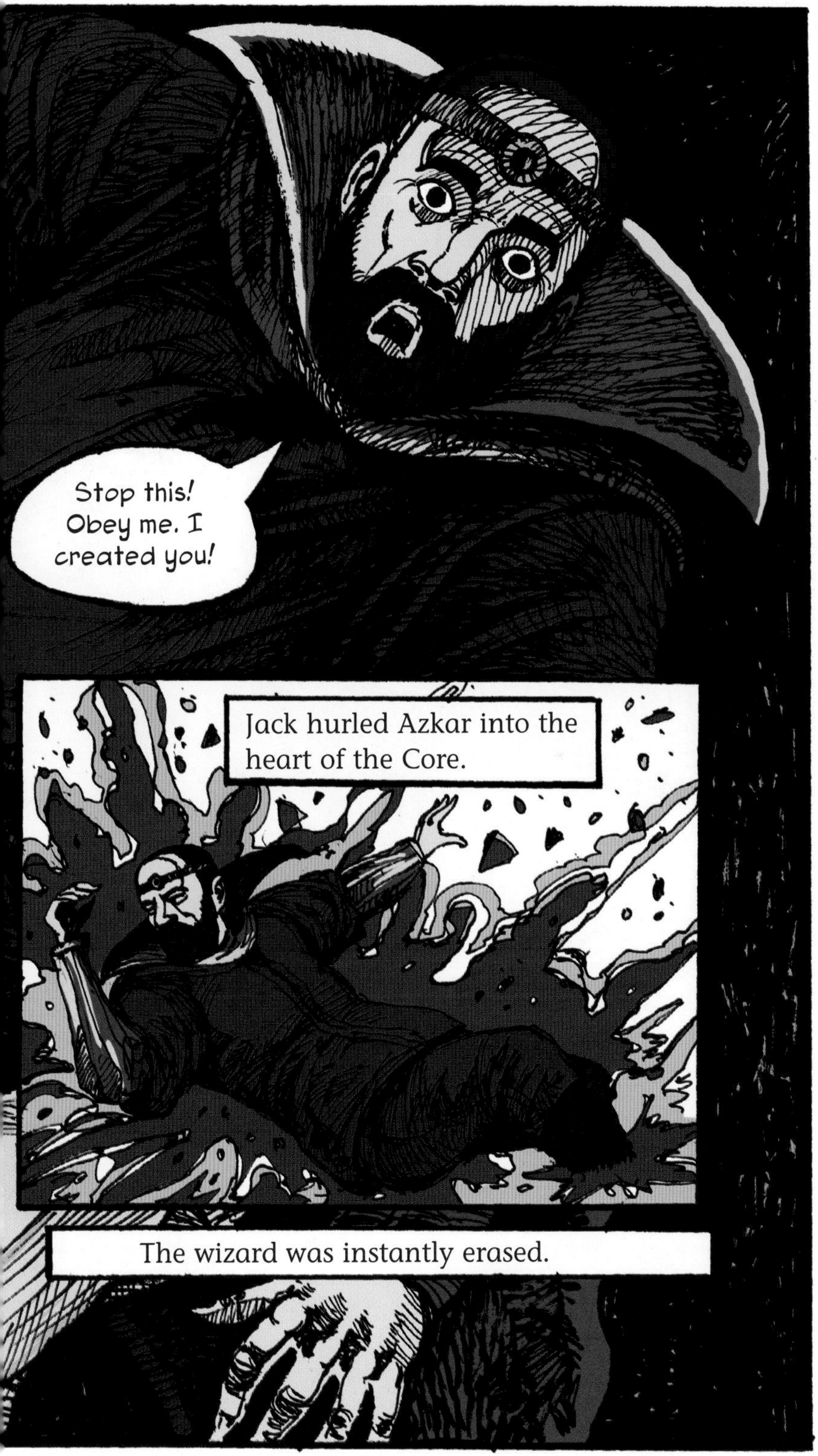
Stop this! Obey me. I created you!
Jack hurled Azkar into the heart of the Core.
The wizard was instantly erased.

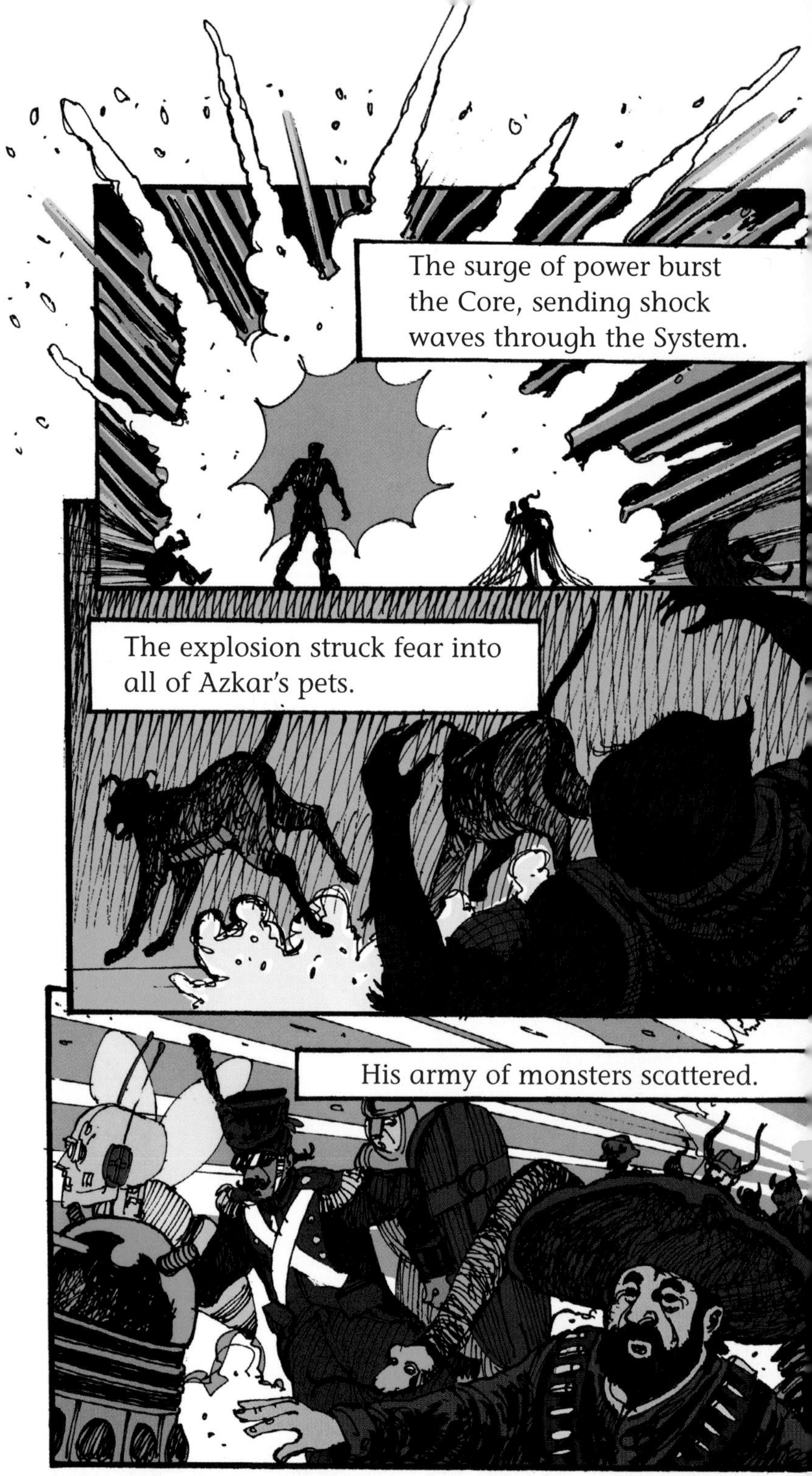
The surge of power burst the Core, sending shock waves through the System.
The explosion struck fear into all of Azkar's pets.
His army of monsters scattered.

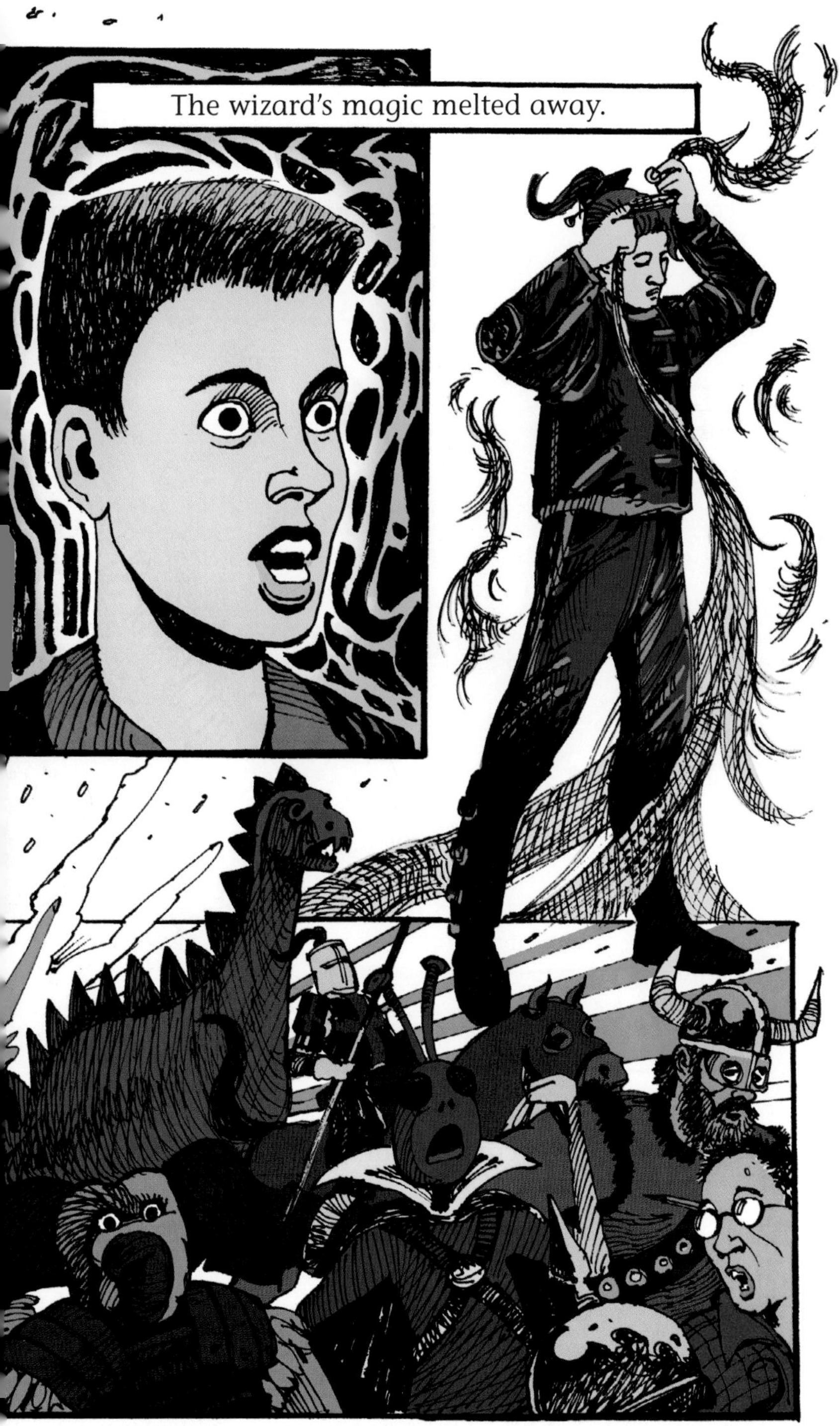
The wizard's magic melted away.

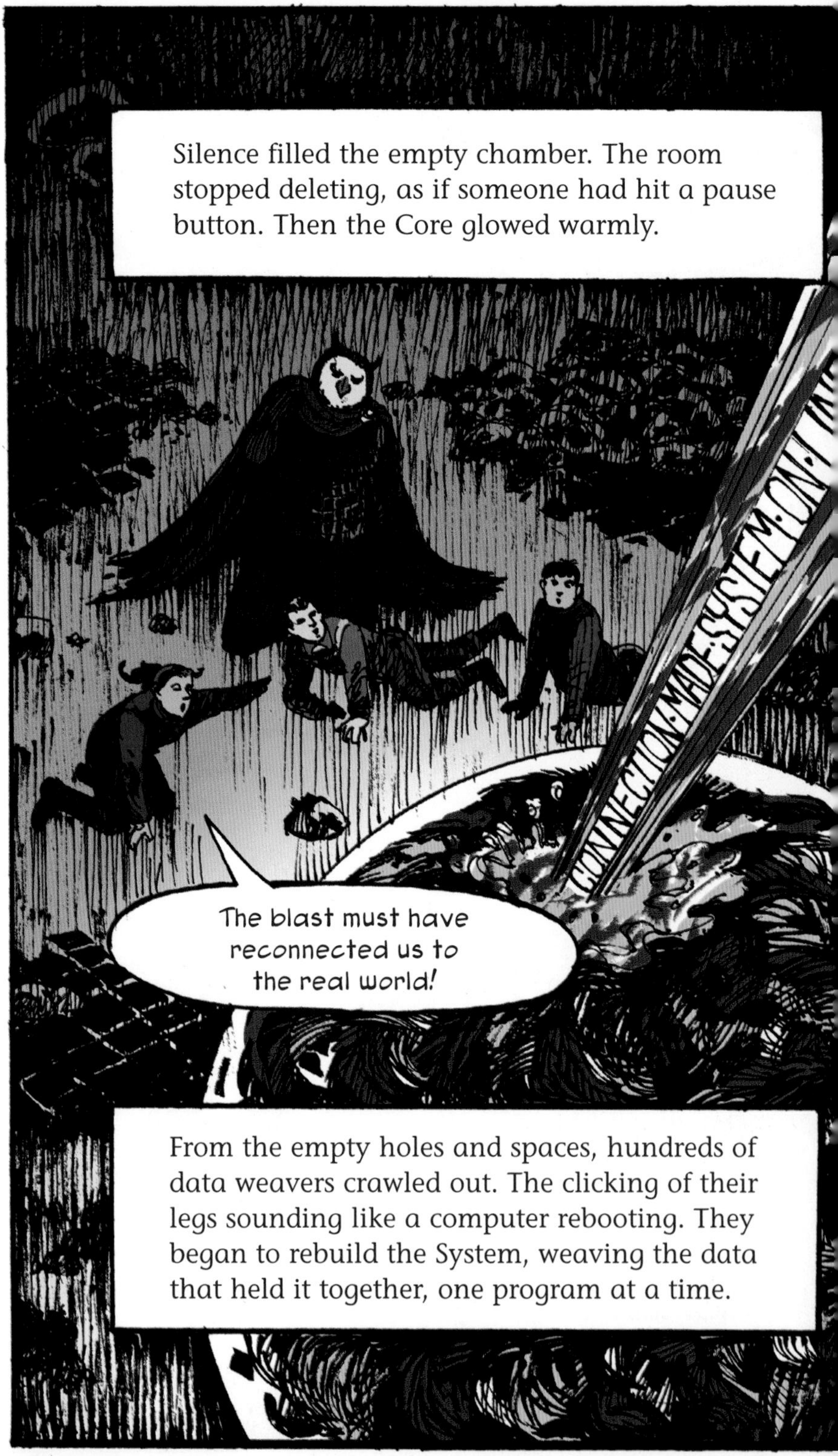
Silence filled the empty chamber. The room stopped deleting, as if someone had hit a pause button. Then the Core glowed warmly.
CONNECTION·MADE·SYSTEM·
The blast must have reconnected us to the real world!
From the empty holes and spaces, hundreds of data weavers crawled out. The clicking of their legs sounding like a computer rebooting. They began to rebuild the System, weaving the data that held it together, one program at a time.

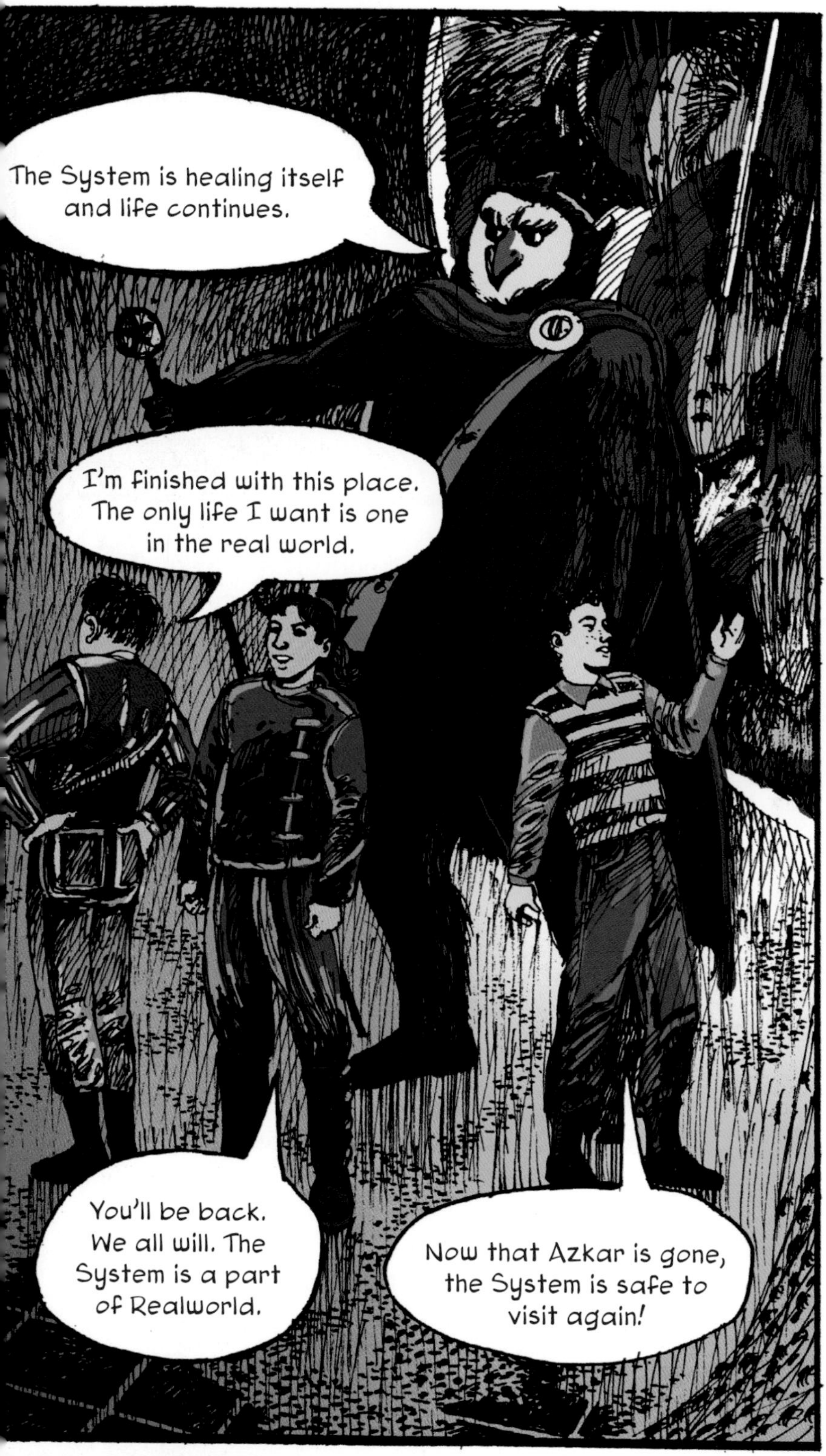
The System is healing itself and life continues.
I'm finished with this place. The only life I want is one in the real world.
You'll be back. We all will. The System is a part of Realworld.
Now that Azkar is gone, the System is safe to visit again!

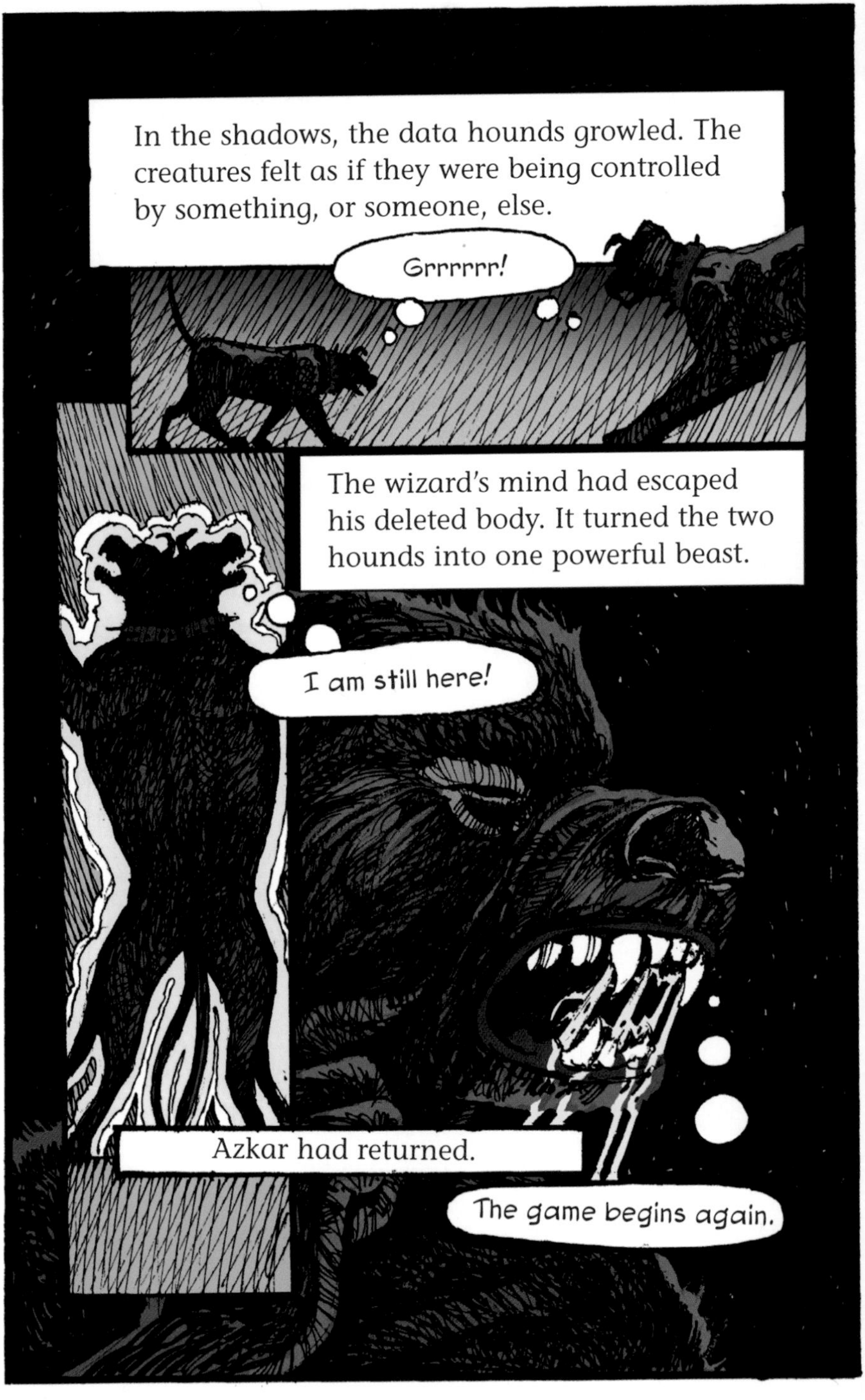
In the shadows, the data hounds growled. The creatures felt as if they were being controlled by something, or someone, else.
Grrrrrr!
The wizard's mind had escaped his deleted body. It turned the two hounds into one powerful beast.
I am still here!
Azkar had returned.
The game begins again.

About the Author

Liam O'Donnell's work has appeared in books, magazines and on television screens across North America and Europe. Liam writes graphic novels and is the creator of Max Finder Mystery, the hit "you-solve-it" comic appearing monthly in *OWL* magazine. He lives in Toronto.

Glossary

boasted (BOHST-id)—bragged

delete (duh-LEET)—to erase or destroy, especially used when getting rid of a computer program

error (ER-ur)—mistake

foundation (foun-DAY-shuhn)—a supporting part; base

looting (LOOT-ing)—stealing, robbing

reboot (ree-BOOT)—to start up a computer

staff (STAF)—a stick or cane carried as an aid in walking or climbing; or a stout stick used as a weapon

vengeance (VEN-juhnss)—with great anger or force

villain (VIL-uhn)—a wicked or evil person

Discussion Questions

1. What is your understanding of the Virtual Reality world? How do Virtual Reality games work? Explain your answers.

2. Jemma does not wait for someone to tell her what to do. If something needs to get done, or someone needs to be saved, she comes to the rescue. What do you think about the type of character she is? Why?

3. When Jack was still the machine man Cyborg, he said "Danny Boy." Why did he say this?

Writing Prompts

1. "Looking strong can lead to problems." Do you agree or disagree with this statement? Explain your answer.

2. During the battle with the strange Olaf (page 47), Daniel thinks, "I can't beat him with strength. I've got to use my brain." How and why does this work or not work for him? Explain your answer.

3. Write a sequel to this story. What happens when Jack and Danny play their video game again? Do they meet any new monsters or villains?

ALSO PUBLISHED BY STONE ARCH BOOKS

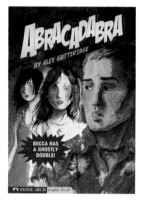

ABRACADABRA
BY ALEX GUTTERIDGE
BECCA HAS A GHOSTLY DOUBLE!
STONE ARCH Graphic Novel

Abracadabra
by Alex Gutteridge

Tom is about to come face-to-face with Charlotte, Becca's double. Tom is confused, though, because Charlotte died more than three hundred years ago.

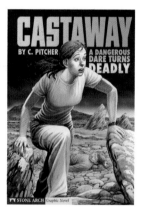

CASTAWAY
BY C. PITCHER
A DANGEROUS DARE TURNS DEADLY
STONE ARCH Graphic Novel

Castaway
by C. Pitcher

Six kids on a geography trip are cut off by the sea. One of them is hurt, it's the middle of the night, and they have only themselves to blame.

HIT IT!
SCOTT'S TEAM IS PLAYING FOR THE CHAMPIONSHIP!
BY MICHAEL HARDCASTLE
STONE ARCH Graphic Novel

Hit It!
by Michael Hardcastle

Scott and Kel are rivals on the same soccer team. What will it take to make them work together?

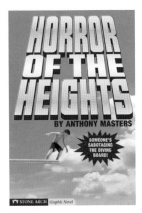

HORROR OF THE HEIGHTS
BY ANTHONY MASTERS
SOMEONE'S SABOTAGING THE DIVING BOARD!
STONE ARCH Graphic Novel

Horror of the Heights
by Anthony Masters

Dean suffers from a fear of heights. That's a big deal when your brother is a diving champion. Now, someone is out to sabotage the diving board that Dean fears. He's got to find out what's going on, for everyone's sake.

Internet Sites

Do you want to know more about subjects related to this book? Or are you interested in learning about other topics? Then check out FactHound, a fun, easy way to find Internet sites.

Our investigative staff has already sniffed out great sites for you!

Here's how to use FactHound:

1. Visit *www.facthound.com*

2. Select your grade level.

3. To learn more about subjects related to this book, type in the book's ISBN number: **1598890832**.

4. Click the **Fetch It** button.

FactHound will fetch the best Internet sites for you.